bully.com

bully.com

Written by
Joe Lawlor

Eerdmans Books for Young Readers
Grand Rapids, Michigan • Cambridge, U.K.

Published 2013 by Eerdmans Books for Young Readers,
an imprint of Wm. B. Eerdmans Publishing Co.
2140 Oak Industrial Dr. NE, Grand Rapids, Michigan 49505
P.O. Box 163, Cambridge CB3 9PU U.K.

www.eerdmans.com/youngreaders

Manufactured at Worzalla, Stevens Point, Wisconsin, USA,
in February 2013; first printing

13 14 15 16 17 18   8 7 6 5 4 3 2 1

Library of Congress Cataloging-in-Publication Data

Lawlor, Joe.
Bully.com / by Joe Lawlor.
pages cm
Summary: Wrongly accused of cyberbullying, seventh-grader Jun Li,
a brilliant student, more comfortable around computers than people,
has seven days to find the real culprit or face explusion.
ISBN 978-0-8028-5413-1
[1. Mystery and detective stories. 2. Cyberbullying — Fiction.
3. Bullying — Fiction. 4. Middle schools — Fiction.
5. Schools — Fiction. 6. Asian Americans — Fiction.]
I. Title.
PZ7.L41886Bu 2013
[Fic] — dc23
2012038990

Cover illustration © 2013 Joshua S. Brunet

For Dee,
who never stopped believing.

Chapter 1

Monday

Jun approached the teacher's desk with short, hesitant steps. In his head, he rehearsed what he would say. It was important not to whine. Teachers hated whiners. Just be honest, he told himself. Mr. Dunne was a reasonable man. Once he recognized the error, he would change the grade. No big deal.

The rest of the class was seated, working quietly. Jun picked his way along the aisle between desks, careful not to step on the books and binders that littered the narrow path. Halfway up the row, an orange-haired girl named Olivia stuck her arm out, barring his way. Jun stumbled to a stop.

"Oh, you're sooo dead," she whispered.

"Huh?" Jun whispered back.

"You heard me."

Olivia held her phone beneath the desk, hidden from the teacher. Jun could see a text displayed on the screen, but it was too small for him to read.

"I-I don't understand," he stammered.

Olivia looked down at the screen and then up at Jun again. Her expression was venomous. "Kimmie's my friend. She's gonna squash you for this."

There was only one Kimmie in the school — Kimmie Cole, a popular girl in the eighth grade. But Jun had never talked to Kimmie. He had never even been in the same room with her.

"I think you've got the wrong guy."

A stern voice from the front of the room ended this whispered exchange.

"Mr. Li?"

It was Mr. Dunne. And he did not look happy.

"Why are you out of your seat?" the teacher asked.

Now was probably not the best time to announce that he wanted his grade changed on last week's test.

"I . . . uh, wanted to talk to you about something."

The teacher frowned. "Then why were you talking to Olivia?"

Jun had hoped to catch Mr. Dunne in a good mood. This was not a promising start.

"I don't know," he answered honestly.

"Have you finished your worksheet?"

Jun nodded. "Five minutes ago."

The teacher looked at the clock, then waved him forward. "We've got a few minutes before the bell."

Jun started toward the front of the class again, glancing once over his shoulder. Olivia was still glaring at him.

What had he done?

At the teacher's desk, Jun pushed the conversation with Olivia to the back of his mind and focused on his original reason for leaving his seat. He shifted his weight from side to side, unsure of how to begin. Up close, Mr. Dunne looked bigger. His shoulders seemed broader, his sandy hair darker, his customary frown deeper.

Mr. Dunne's eyes settled on the paper clenched in Jun's hand.

"Is that last week's test?" he asked.

Jun held out the paper, his hand trembling. "I think you may have marked something wrong." That sounded too forward, so he quickly added, "Accidentally, of course."

Grimacing, the teacher accepted the test from Jun and laid it on his desk. The corner where Jun had held the paper was rumpled. Using the palm of his hand, Mr. Dunne ironed out the wrinkles.

"Page four." Jun reached across the desk to turn the page and bumped hands with Mr. Dunne making the same move. "Sorry," Jun said, snatching back his hand.

Mr. Dunne gave him a sour look but said nothing.

"Right there," Jun said, motioning with his chin. "I wrote *King Tutankhaten* and you marked it wrong."

"That's because it *is* wrong," Mr. Dunne said. "The correct answer is *King Tutankhamun*. Spelling counts."

"I know," Jun said, "but I believe my answer is correct as well. I looked it up online."

"Jun," Mr. Dunne said with whispered exasperation, "you can't always trust what you find on the internet."

Jun expected this argument. "I'm pretty sure this information is correct. I have confirmation from a reliable source."

Mr. Dunne leaned back and folded his arms. "From whom?"

"I traded emails with Professor Hardy. He told me that both answers were acceptable."

Mr. Dunne's eyebrows rose. "Professor William Hardy? From Columbia University?"

"You mentioned his name in class a few weeks back. He was your college professor, right? I remember seeing his book on your shelf." Even without glancing up, Jun knew where the book resided. Third shelf, a quarter of the way down on the left side. "Anyway, Professor Hardy said the king was originally named Tutankhaten. It was the priests that changed the name to Tutankhamun, after Amun, the god of Thebes. So you see," Jun said with a nervous laugh, "both answers are correct."

Mr. Dunne did not look amused.

Jun fished a slip of paper out of his pocket and handed it to the teacher. "I wrote down Professor Hardy's email address. You can check with him if you want."

The teacher waved the paper away. "That won't be necessary." Mr. Dunne studied the test, then looked up at Jun again. "Why didn't you just talk to me about this?"

Jun didn't know what to say. He had wanted to confirm his facts before confronting the teacher. Was that so wrong?

"I don't know," he muttered.

Mr. Dunne reached for a red pen. "I'll change your grade, Jun. But I can't say I like the way you went about this. You're a seventh grader now. If you've got a problem, you need to speak with me face-to-face."

Mr. Dunne crossed out the old grade and wrote the new one using extra-large numbers. The oversized grade, combined with the teacher's criticism, made Jun wish he'd never left his seat.

The bell rang. Binders snapped shut, papers were stuffed into folders, and chairs scraped across the tile floor as Jun's classmates pressed toward the door.

Jun backed away from the teacher's desk, holding up the test.

"Thanks for this," he said.

Mr. Dunne replied with a half-hearted wave.

Turning, Jun spotted Olivia exiting the class. He followed after her, wanting more details about her accusation. It was crazy, wasn't it? In what alternate dimension could his name be mixed up with Kimmie Cole's?

By the time he reached the doorway, Olivia had disappeared into the heavy traffic flowing to block two. Jun scanned the crowd for her orange hair, but there was no sign of her.

Chris Pine, his next-door neighbor and best friend, strode toward Mr. Dunne's classroom. Unlike Olivia, she was easy to spot. Chris was the tallest kid in the seventh grade. Jun was just the opposite. His mother was Japanese and his father Chinese. Their combined genetic material guaranteed he'd always be picked last for basketball. Adding an inch to his height were three spiky tufts of black hair that stuck up on the back of his head. His father often joked that Jun styled his hair with a wet finger and an electrical socket.

Chris studied his face. "You alright?"

Jun wanted to explain, but the harder he searched for the words to describe his encounter with Olivia, the more trivial it seemed.

She had the wrong guy. That was that.

"I'm fine," he said, starting down the hall. "I just had a weird conversation with Mr. Dunne."

"About what?" Chris said, falling into step beside him.

"I asked him to change my grade on Thursday's test."

"I thought you got a hundred on that test," Chris said.

"I did, but I didn't get all the questions right."

"How can you get a hundred and not get all the questions right?"

"This was the bonus question."

"You were arguing over the bonus?" Chris shook her head. "That's so you."

"Private school applications are due next month," Jun said. "And I just got the catalog for Wellington. Get this — next year they're offering a course in video-game design!"

"Thrilling," Chris said without enthusiasm. She tucked a few strands of her long brown hair behind her ear. The rest was tied in a long ponytail that swished back and forth across the white numbers on her Celtics jersey. "I'm coming over to your house after school today, okay?"

Chris often issued commands that only masqueraded as questions.

"Um . . . sure," Jun said, "but don't you have basketball?"

"Coach Brown's got the flu. Practice is cancelled until he's back." Chris sidestepped a kid tying his shoe in the middle of the hall. "It'll be fun. We'll do homework or something."

Chris volunteering to do homework was like a wild turkey offering to hop directly into the oven. "Everything alright?" he asked.

Chris shrugged. "My aunt's getting married this week-end, and mom is making me get my hair cut."

That didn't sound so terrible.

"You need a haircut," Jun answered honestly.

Chris whacked him across the shoulder. She was solidly built, so her hand landed with more of a *thud* than a *smack*.

"What?" he said, rubbing his arm. "It's true."

"Yeah, I know it's true," Chris said. "But that doesn't mean I want to hear you say it out loud." She shook her head. "The haircut isn't the problem. Mom's taking me to the salon for a manicure and pedicure, too."

"You say that like it's the end of the world."

"I don't like strangers touching my feet."

Jun grinned. "Are you ticklish?"

Chris glared down at him. Her narrowed eyes informed him that the starting center for the 4-and-0 Hornets could never be ticklish.

Chris stopped suddenly. She stuck her arm out, forcing Jun to stop, too. "Um . . . is it just me or are people staring at us?"

Jun scanned the hall. She was right. Pockets of kids stood beside their lockers and in doorways, whispering and pointing at them.

Jun studied the angle of their extended fingers.

Correction: they were pointing at *him*!

On an average day, Jun attracted about as much attention as the pencils and crumpled papers that littered the edges of the hallway. Jun spotted phones cupped furtively in the hands of at least four of his classmates, and Olivia's bizarre accusation washed over him again. He wished now that he'd been able to read that text.

His attention snapped back to center as a stocky eighth grader approached and planted himself in front of Jun. His thick black eyebrows pulled together, forming a straight line across his forehead.

"Are you Jun Li?" he asked through clenched teeth.

"Uh . . . yeah," Jun said, taking a half step back. "That's me."

The kid grabbed two fistfuls of Jun's shirt, spun him a quarter turn, and slammed him into the lockers. Jun's shoulders hit first, followed by his head, which set his ears ringing. The eighth grader got in Jun's face. "You thought I wouldn't figure it out, huh? You thought you could get away with it."

Jun was too stunned to reply. The kid's face swam in and out of focus. It took five rapid blinks for the double images to merge.

Grimacing and rubbing his head, Jun asked, "What's going on?"

"Like you don't know."

Chris inserted herself between them, forcing the eighth grader to release his hold.

Jun peeked around Chris's shoulder for a better look at his attacker. Now he recognized the kid — Jun had seen his picture in the local paper. His name was Charlie . . . something. He'd been the top scorer last week in a lacrosse game against Dedham.

Jun fell back on the only weapon he had — his vocabulary. "I can see you're upset, but perhaps you can better articulate what's making you so irate."

"Huh?" Charlie said.

Chris translated, "He wants to know why you're so pissed off!"

"I just came from the office," Charlie said. "I know it was you."

"What are you talking about? I didn't do anything!"

Charlie started nodding, like he should have expected this tactic. "Yeah, that's right. Play dumb."

Jun glanced at Chris to make sure he wasn't missing anything. She looked just as confused.

"Kimmie's a mess," Charlie went on. "I was on the phone with her all last night."

There was that name again. What had happened to Kimmie? Actually, the more pressing question was — what did Charlie think *he* had done to her?

Jun shook his head in helpless bewilderment.

Charlie wasn't convinced. "Drop the act. I know you posted those pictures."

"What pictures? Posted them where?"

A bell chimed from an unseen overhead speaker. "Jun Li, please report to the office. Jun Li to the office."

Charlie smiled. His teeth, like his body, were square and blocky. "Now you're going to get it. And when the principal's done with you," Charlie tapped a finger against his broad chest, "it'll be my turn."

Charlie spun on his heel and strode off, arms at his sides, fists clenched, leading with his shoulder to cut through the small ring of kids that had gathered to watch the drama.

"What was *that* all about?" Chris asked.

Jun thought back to his encounter with Olivia. Five minutes ago, it all seemed like a big misunderstanding. A case of mistaken identity. But now the office was involved. The trouble was real. Whatever was going on, it was serious. Call-your-mother serious.

"I don't know," he said, looking over his shoulder in the direction of the office. "But I guess I'm about to find out."

Chapter 2

After the commotion in the hallway, the office felt still and library-quiet. Jun closed the door carefully behind him and crossed the thin blue carpet to the reception desk. He'd been in the office only once before. That had been at the end of sixth grade when he had picked up his certificate for perfect attendance. Given what had just happened in the hallway, Jun was pretty sure that this time there would be no award.

Mrs. Kwon, the office receptionist, was pressing a folder into the top drawer of an overstuffed filing cabinet.

"Excuse me," Jun said, stopping at her desk. "I think there's been some sort of mistake. I was just called down."

Mrs. Kwon gave one final push and the folder slid into place. Over her shoulder, she asked, "Are you Jun Li?"

He nodded.

"Mr. Hastings wants to see you right away." She pointed down a side corridor.

This was bad. Each grade level had a team leader that was in charge of discipline. If you were in *really* big trouble, you were sent to the vice principal's office. The principal, as far as Jun knew, only dealt with expulsions and incidents that made the front page of the *Brookfield Times*.

Jun started down the corridor. He reached for the first knob on the right.

"Not that one," Mrs. Kwon said. "Further down. On your left."

"Sorry. It's my first time." He managed a smile, letting her know that there wasn't much chance a kid like him could be in any real trouble.

She nodded, but her large, dark eyes looked worried. She knew something that he didn't and that something, whatever it was, made the blueberry muffin in his stomach turn somersaults. He rubbed the lump on the back of his head. The throb had been replaced by an itchy sting.

Jun knocked on the open door of the principal's office. "Excuse me?"

Principal Hastings looked up. He had silver hair and a long, thin face interrupted by a pair of glasses. A second set of glasses hung from a strap around his neck. Mr. Hastings was new to the school this year. Jun had seen him a few times before, mostly in the auditorium. He didn't re-member much about the man, except that he was the only administrator who didn't need a microphone to address all four hundred students in the seventh grade.

The principal took one look at Jun and shouted past him, "Mrs. Kwon!"

It wasn't an angry shout, but the sheer volume of it made Jun fall back a step. Mrs. Kwon's soft voice replied through the intercom.

"Yes, Mr. Hastings?"

"I told you to send me June," he shouted back through the door.

"That is Jun," the intercom replied.

Mr. Hastings squinted, then changed his glasses, let-ting the first pair drop around his neck.

"You're June?"

His mother had named him after his great-grandfather, a well-respected physician. Jun had never met his name-sake, but he was pretty sure the other Jun, the one who lived and worked all his life in Osaka, never had to deal with being mistaken for a girl.

Jun spelled out his name for the principal. When that seemed insufficient, he added, "My name means truthful."

"Truthful, huh?"

The note of doubt in the principal's voice made Jun's confusion complete.

Mr. Hastings extended a hand to an empty chair in front of his desk. Jun lowered himself onto the edge of the seat. For several seconds, the only sounds in the room were the hum of the radiator and the soft *whoosh-whoosh-whoosh* of traffic that raced past the school.

Arms folded, Mr. Hastings waited for him to say something.

Jun's tongue felt thick and heavy. "I'm a little confused," he managed. "I was just attacked by this eighth grader I don't even know. And then I got called down here."

"The eighth grader must be Charlie Bruno," the principal said. "He came into my office halfway through block one, complaining about the situation with Kimmie."

"You mean Kimmie Cole?" Jun asked.

"Yes. She's Charlie's girlfriend, so I'm not surprised he went after you."

If *America's Next Top Model* had a middle school edition, Kimmie Cole would be on it. She was that put together. Charlie . . . well, with the caterpillar eyebrows and the fire-hydrant physique, his face was better suited to radio. The two went together like caviar and peanut butter.

A copy of Jun's sixth-grade report card lay open on the desk. The principal looked down at it, then back up at Jun. "You're a smart boy," he said. "Maybe you can tell me why I've called you in today."

"Really," Jun said earnestly, "I don't know."

Mr. Hastings nodded as if that was exactly the response he expected to hear. He leaned back in his chair; his fingers formed a steeple as he mulled over his next words. "Perhaps you can tell me what you were doing in the school library during block seven on Friday?"

Jun's stomach sank into his sneakers.

On Friday he'd emailed Professor Hardy. Jun knew he'd been right about King Tut. He'd been right and Mr. Dunne had been wrong and it hadn't taken more than a few emails to prove it for sure. But Jun should have waited until he arrived home. Accessing personal email accounts at school was forbidden because it required slipping around the filtering system. Still, it was a minor offense. It couldn't be the reason Jun now sat in the principal's office. Jun studied the creases that radiated from Mr. Hastings's narrowed eyes. Could it?

Mr. Hastings opened a file folder and slid a stapled packet across the desktop. Kimmie Cole, dressed in her yellow and black field hockey uniform, stared up at him from the first page. Above the picture were the words:

Want to look gorgeous just like me?

"That's a printout of the pictures and text that were posted Friday afternoon," Mr. Hastings said. "Go on. Read it."

Jun picked the packet up and thumbed through the

first few pages. They were formatted the same as the first, but the pictures grew more disturbing the deeper he got into the packet. He stopped before the end and set the packet carefully on the desk, like it might explode if he put it down too quickly.

Jun could see why Charlie Bruno was upset. The pictures informed the world that Kimmie maintained her slender figure, not by diet and exercise, but by sticking her finger down her throat. Maybe that was why he was here. Maybe Mr. Hastings needed his assistance in tracking down the cyberbully.

"Where was this posted?" Jun asked.

"On the school's website. It was the first thing the superintendent saw when he logged in this morning. Most of his coffee ended up in his lap."

"I think I can help," Jun said confidently, "but I'll need access to your server."

Mr. Hastings's response was something between a laugh and a snort. "I don't want your help," he said. "What I want is to know is why *you* posted those pictures!"

Jun's head snapped back. Whatever he'd been expecting, whatever he'd imagined the principal might accuse him of, exposing Kimmie Cole's eating disorder was not among the possibilities.

"I have witnesses that say they saw *you* post these pictures."

"But I don't even know Kimmie Cole," Jun said.

"You know her last name."

"Everyone *knows* Kimmie."

If you made a list of the most dangerous forces in the world, Kimmie would probably be somewhere in the top ten, sandwiched between global warming and nuclear war. If Kimmie had a problem with you, she wouldn't bother whispering about you behind your back or writing nasty things about your mother on the bathroom wall. Kimmie embarrassed you online so your humiliation could be witnessed by every person with internet access — around two billion, worldwide.

This time, it seemed, someone had beaten Kimmie at her own game.

"Just because I know who she is," Jun said, "doesn't mean I posted those pictures."

"I didn't just pick your name out of a hat," Mr. Hastings said. "I checked with Mr. Jolinski, our tech support manager. He was able to pinpoint when the pictures were posted and from what computer in the library. And the librarian says she saw you breaking through the school's firewall during the timeframe Mr. Jolinski specified. The obvious conclusion is . . ."

Jun held up a hand, interrupting. He couldn't help making a tiny clarification. "The firewall keeps people from breaking in. The school's filtering system is what blocks restricted sites, like email."

The principal nodded slowly. "Seems like you know a lot about computers."

Jun pursed his lips and sank lower in his chair.

Mr. Hastings set his elbows on the desk. "This is what it comes down to. Somehow, you got around the . . . the *filtering system* on Friday and posted those pictures."

"Okay, I did sneak around the filter," Jun admitted, "but I didn't hack into the school's website and I did not post any pictures!"

"Then what were you doing on that computer?"

"Trying to improve my social studies grade." It was a statement, but it came out like more of a question. He went on to explain about exchanging emails with Professor Hardy, the Columbia University professor.

"Mr. Dunne will confirm this?"

Jun nodded.

"And what was your final grade?"

Jun looked down at his knees, embarrassed.

"Well?"

"One hundred and five," Jun muttered.

"Come again?"

"One hundred and five," he said, louder.

The principal's forehead wrinkled with confusion.

"It was the bonus question," Jun explained.

"You argued over the bonus?"

Jun shrugged, not understanding why he felt so ashamed. Wasn't the point of school to get good grades? Did he really need to explain that to the principal?

Mr. Hastings changed glasses again as he thumbed through Jun's file. While the papers shuffled, Jun looked out the window. A light rain fell, too thin to be seen. Windshield wipers swept back and forth on the cars that zipped past the school.

Refocusing his eyes, he saw his own ghostly reflection in the window. Jun cursed himself for sending that email on Friday. Why couldn't he have waited until he got home? Was all the trouble he was in right now really worth five measly points?

Mr. Hastings looked up. "Your disciplinary records are clean, Jun. But that doesn't change the facts. You were spotted at the same computer from which the pictures were posted. That, combined with your obvious computer skills, makes you a suspect."

Jun thought about his applications. He was pretty sure Wellington, the state's most prestigious private school, didn't accept cyberbullies, even the ones that earned straight As.

"What if I find out who's really behind this?" Jun said.

The principal's eyebrows arched. "Why would I let my only suspect investigate?"

"Because I know computers," Jun said quickly. "I know

the difference between firewalls and filtering systems. And I know that posting those pictures on Friday probably didn't take more than five minutes."

The principal flipped through the packet. "How can that be?"

"The pictures and text were probably created ahead of time, then uploaded to the school's website *after* the cyber-bully slipped around the filtering system. The tricky part would be gaining access to the school's website. The culprit must have hacked the administrator's password."

Mr. Hastings absorbed Jun's theory with a slow nod. After a pause for consideration, he said, "Kimmie's mother, Mrs. Cole, wants this handled quietly. She's worried that if she files a report with the police, her daughter's face will pop up on the local news every five minutes. She's given me a week to find the cyberbully before she contacts the police."

"Which is exactly why you need me!" Jun said, gripping the edge of the principal's desk. "Kids might tell me things they wouldn't say to the principal."

Mr. Hastings studied Jun's report card again. After half a minute, which felt like half an hour to Jun, the principal looked up. "I've only just begun my investigation. You've got until Monday to clear your name. If you don't have any new information by then, I'll have to take immediate action."

Jun didn't like the sound of that.

Mr. Hastings explained, "This isn't the first time cyberbullying has been a problem at this school. As a result, the school board instituted a zero-tolerance policy this year. Once the guilty party is found, and the evidence is confirmed, he or she will be expelled."

It was all happening too fast for Jun to process. "You mean I could be kicked out of school?"

Mr. Hasting removed his glasses. "Your record has bought you a few days, Jun. Use the time to find the cyberbully."

The principal wrote Jun a pass.

Jun accepted it with a shaking hand. "But what about Charlie Bruno?"

"I'll take care of Mr. Bruno," the principal assured him. "Just get to the bottom of this. By Monday."

Chapter 3

Jun sat through his next four classes in a daze. One hundred and fifty-nine minutes of instruction, and Jun couldn't remember a single detail about the pharaohs of Ancient Egypt or how to divide a whole number by a fraction. Nor could he wrap his brain around the idea that he had until Monday — just seven short days — to find the cyberbully.

Jun walked to the cafeteria with his head down. He didn't like talking to strangers. He even avoided answering the door when the pizza-delivery guy rang the bell. And now he was expected to interview teachers, librarians, and students? Not a chance!

Jun pulled open the cafeteria door and joined the end of the hot-lunch line. The day's menu offered the usual fare: rubbery hot dogs, watery vegetables, and that unnaturally colored cheese they drizzled over the nachos. Oddly enough, Jun found the cafeteria's sounds and smells somewhat comforting. They were familiar, part of the usual routine on a day that was 180 degrees from normal.

As Jun shuffled down the aisle between tables, heads turned. News of his trip to the principal's office had clearly made a few laps around the school. Some of the looks he received were admiring, clearly broadcasting their happiness that someone had *finally* stood up to Kimmie. Other kids — Kimmie's friends, no doubt — shot death rays in Jun's direction. Either way, he was getting the credit or the blame for something he didn't do.

He took his usual seat in the back corner, and huddled his narrow frame behind his blue lunch bag, trying to ignore the unwanted attention. He pulled his lunch from the bag, placing the apple on the opposite side of the table for Chris. He set the sandwich aside, too, in favor of the cake. He unwrapped it quickly and devoured the chocolate triangle in four big bites. The sugar rush loosened the knot in his stomach.

"Don't forget to breathe," Chris said, plunking herself down across from him.

"Where . . ." Crumbs flew from his mouth. He drew his forearm across his lips. "Where have you been?" he asked again, noting that Chris was five minutes later than usual.

"I couldn't get into the girls' bathroom. I had to use

the one all the way over by the nurse's office." She picked up the apple Jun had left for her and rubbed it against her green jersey. "All the girls were jammed in the bathroom, trying to get a look at Kimmie's pictures on their phones."

Kimmie's name counteracted the soothing effects of the cake.

"Guess who the principal thinks is behind the pictures?" Jun pointed a finger at his chest.

"Yeah, I heard," Chris said, starting to laugh.

"What's so funny?"

She tried, unsuccessfully, to straighten her smile. "Nothing."

Already that morning, he'd been attacked by Charlie Bruno and accused of a crime he didn't commit. Having his best friend laugh at him — not helping.

"What?" he demanded.

"It's just . . . you're the last person in the world that would do something like that."

"The principal doesn't think so." Jun filled Chris in on the details of the meeting.

A sharp snap followed as Chris's teeth sank through the apple's skin. She chewed thoughtfully. "So what happens if you can't find her by Monday?"

"Then Mr. Hastings . . ." Jun stopped, tilting his head to one side. "Wait. How do you know it's a *her*?"

Chris shrugged. "I don't know. But boys are more

in-your-face, you know? Girls tend to be sneakier. They stick the knife in your back, not your chest."

Jun raised a finger to object. "But Mr. Hastings called *me* down to the office first."

"Didn't he did think you were a girl?"

"Good point," Jun conceded.

"So?" Chris pressed. "What happens if you can't find out who it was by Monday?"

The words bubbled up to his mouth. Jun held onto them for a long as he could, fearing that if he spoke them out loud it would increase the chance they'd come true. "Mr. Hastings said he'd kick me out of school."

Chris's jaw dropped, and Jun could see a chunk of half-chewed apple. "That's CRAZY!" she shouted. "You didn't do ANYTHING!"

Chris's reaction pleased him. He wished she'd been with him in the principal's office. What she lacked in diplomacy, she made up for in volume.

Jun explained about the new zero-tolerance policy.

"Don't they need proof or something before they boot you out of school?" Chris asked.

"I know how to get around the filtering system, *and* I was spotted at the same computer those pictures were posted." Jun shook his head. "I'm innocent, but even *I'm* not sure I believe me."

***

After the final bell, Jun and Chris went to see Mr. Jolinski, the school's technical support manager. Jun needed to examine the pictures more carefully. The preview he'd gotten in Mr. Hastings's office didn't count. He'd been too nervous to do a thorough inspection. He hoped that seeing the pictures on a computer screen, the way they were intended to be viewed, might yield some fresh clues.

Jun knocked.

A large, balding man opened the door. Pictures of sailboats and palm trees dotted his blue Hawaiian shirt. A stubby, blond ponytail held by a blue rubber band stuck out from the back of his head.

Mr. Jolinski looked to Chris. "You must be June," he said. "The principal said you'd be stopping by."

"*I'm* Jun," Jun said, pressing a hand to his chest. He considered wearing a nametag to school. Not that it would help. Chris was so tall people always looked to her first.

"Sorry. I didn't know . . . "

"It's okay," Chris interrupted. "People confuse us all the time, you know, because we look so much alike."

Mr. Jolinski chuckled. "A regular pair of twins."

"Um, can we take a look at the pictures?" Jun asked. He was eager to begin the process of clearing his good name. Whatever was left of it, at least.

"Come on in."

Jun followed Mr. Jolinski's ponytail into a room lined

with metal storage racks. The shelves were filled with laptops, power strips, keyboards, mice, and a hopeless tangle of wires and cables. With several computers running at once, the room was warmer than the hall, despite the small air conditioner humming in the back window.

Jun picked up a motherboard and turned it over in his hands. "Mr. Jolinski, if you ever have a garage sale . . ."

"You wouldn't want it. This is the PC burial ground where hard drives come to die." Mr. Jolinski sat down behind his desk in the far corner. The man's thick fingers moved surprisingly fast over the keyboard.

Jun crossed to the desk. An open bag of potato chips lay beside the computer. "Help yourself," Mr. Jolinski said, when he saw Jun eyeing the bag. "My wife has me on a diet, and those aren't on it."

Jun didn't need to be asked twice. He grabbed a handful of chips. Chewing helped him focus.

"Okay," Mr. Jolinski began, "I took the photos down this morning. What you're about to see is just a copy."

Jun stepped behind Mr. Jolinski's chair for a better view of the screen. Plastered over the banner that read "Brookfield Middle School" was same line of text Jun had seen in the packet.

"Want to look gorgeous just like me?"

Kimmie's field hockey picture followed. She had her stick raised over her head, lifting her Hornets T-shirt enough to expose her belly button and the bottom half of her ribs. Even Jun, who was on the skinny side, winced when he saw her ribcage. She was skin and bones.

"Oh, that's attractive," Chris said.

Mr. Jolinski scrolled down to reveal the next line of text.

First, you need to eat this.

A picture of a cheeseburger followed. The meat was so thick a person would need a snake's detachable jaw to take the first bite.

And you should eat this too.

Mr. Jolinski scrolled down and a gigantic sundae with chocolate syrup and cherries filled the screen. A kid could easily exceed his or her daily calorie allotment just by looking at it.

And this.

In the next picture, multicolored bowls filled with cranberries, mashed potatoes, and stuffing surrounded an enormous golden-brown turkey on an oval platter.

When you're done, visit here.

A white toilet filled the screen.

And do this.

The next picture was of a girl with her head in the toilet. The picture made Jun feel pukey.

And this.

It was another picture of a girl vomiting. Different girl. Different toilet. Still gross.

And this.

This one showed a blond-headed girl resting her cheek on the toilet seat. Her eyes were pinched shut and her mouth gaped. Jun guessed this was the "after" picture. There was something about seeing the girl's cheek on the toilet seat that grossed him out more than the puking itself.

If you do all this, then you can look gorgeous just like me.

The final picture was the same as the first. This time Jun

was even more disturbed by Kimmie's stick-figure appearance.

"What time was this posted?" he asked.

Mr. Jolinski's fingers tap-danced on the keyboard. "According to this, 1:46 p.m."

"I was off that computer by 1:40," Jun muttered to himself. He tried unsuccessfully to recall who had been on the computer after him. As far as he could remember, the station had remained empty.

"So that's it, right?" Chris said to Jun. "All we have to do is look up who logged onto the computer after you."

"Jun didn't use his login," Mr. Jolinski said, "and neither did the person who posted those pictures. There's a generic login and password that anyone can use. No one's *supposed* to know about it."

Despite the sharp words, Jun thought he detected the hint of a smile at the corners of Mr. Jolinski's mouth. Perhaps the tech support manager was hiding some geeky appreciation for Jun's hacking abilities.

"But why did the cyberbully post this from the school library?" Chris asked. "Wouldn't it have been safer to do it from home?"

Mr. Jolinski leaned back in his chair. "A public place isn't a bad idea," he said. "Often these pictures can be traced back to the computers they were posted from. If you send it from a school library, you've got a thousand possible suspects."

"One thousand one hundred and twelve to be exact," Jun said.

Mr. Jolinski and Chris exchanged glances. They looked at Jun with eyebrows raised.

"What?" Jun said, surprised by the sudden attention. "It's on the school website."

When neither responded, Jun shrugged. Numbers had a way of sticking to his brain the way gum does to hair. It was a gift. That's what his father told him. So why were Chris and Mr. Jolinski looking at him like he'd just sprouted a third eyeball? Jun decided to ignore it.

"Okay," he said, "I'll need a list of all the students in the library at that time." He could picture how things would play out from here. Once he had the list, one of the names on it had to be the bully. It might take some time, but Jun was confident that by Monday he could track down the culprit. He crunched two more chips. "I'll also need to speak with the librarian."

"Mrs. Adams is out sick," Mr. Jolinski said. "She's got that bug that's going around. The only adult in the library at that time was Mrs. Dent. She's a parent volunteer."

"Where can I find her?"

"Do I look like the personnel department?" Mr. Jolinski asked. "Ask Mrs. Kwon. She'll know."

"Alright, thanks," Jun said, striding to the door. Chris didn't follow. When he'd reached the hall and turned, he found that she was giving him those big eyes that meant he'd done something wrong.

What now?

Jun looked down. Mr. Jolinski's potato chip bag was still cradled in his arm. Head hanging low, Jun shuffled back to Mr. Jolinski and handed over the bag.

Mr. Jolinski took the bag and reached inside. He found nothing but crumbs. His long face bunched into a frown.

"I'm, I'm, I'm . . ." Jun started.

"What he's trying to say is that he'll buy you another bag," Chris said.

"And I'll get the baked kind," Jun added. "They're supposed to have fewer calories."

Chris winced. "We *really* need to be going." She seized Jun's hand and dragged him to the doorway.

"Thanks again for your help," Jun said before Chris yanked him into the hall.

Chapter 4

"I can't believe you ate the whole bag," Chris said as they pushed out of the school's double doors.

"It was already half empty. Besides, he said to help myself."

"He didn't mean for you to eat the whole thing."

"I was hungry."

"You're always hungry." Chris counted on her fingers. "Before school. After school. Before dinner. After dinner. Before bed."

"Can I help it if I have a healthy appetite?" he asked.

Chris snorted. "I've seen what you eat. There's nothing *healthy* about your appetite." She stopped at the corner. "Which way?"

Before leaving school, Jun had spoken with Mrs. Kwon.

The receptionist informed him that Mrs. Dent worked as a hair stylist at Hair Razors, located on Washington Street about a half mile from school. Jun pointed to the right and they started off again. The rain he'd seen through Mr. Hastings's window that morning had stopped. The still-wet sidewalks glimmered with the light from the sun that hovered above a bed of grey clouds.

"What did you think of the pictures?" Jun asked.

"I've seen fatter skeletons."

"Any idea who might be behind it?"

"Don't ask me. If I've got a problem with somebody, I don't hide behind a computer. I get right in their face, you know? Tell 'em what's on my mind."

"Big surprise there," Jun said, grinning.

"I'm being serious. Posting nasty stuff is the coward's way out."

Jun wondered what he'd do in the same situation. He didn't have a black belt in karate, couldn't swing a bat, and the most exercise he got came from waving his arms in front of his motion-controlled video games. So if someone decided to pick on him, what could he do? Hit the bully over the head with his Xbox?

"Those pictures . . ." Chris continued. "I know it was mean and all, but you gotta admit — Kimmie had it coming. You remember what she did to Rachel Cook?"

Jun wished he didn't. Whatever Rachel Cook had done

to make Kimmie mad, Jun didn't know, but in retaliation Kimmie had taken a picture of Rachel in the girls' locker room. Some images, once glimpsed, branded themselves onto your brain. Rachel had been in the process of taking off her shirt. The top half of the picture captured part of Rachel's face as seen through her crisscrossed arms. The majority of the photo, however, focused on her stomach. Rachel was a big girl and the sight of her bulging belly was less than flattering. The picture was posted on Facebook with a headline that read AND THAT'S HER GOOD SIDE.

The fact that he was helping Kimmie, the school's worst bully, made Jun uneasy. But what could he do? The only way to keep his name out of the papers — and his butt in school — was to find the cyberbully.

"There it is," Chris said, pointing to a narrow building sandwiched between a deli and a laundromat. *Hair Razors* was written in gold type on the window. Beneath it, a giant pair of scissors and a comb crisscrossed like dueling swords.

A silver convertible was parked beside the curb. Jun and Chris walked around it and pushed through the glass door. A woman with wavy blond hair sat behind the reception desk. Her feet were up as she filed her long fingernails. She wore pink sweatpants and a zip-up hoodie with the word *Pretty* stitched into the fabric across her chest.

Jun crossed to the desk, eager to get some answers.

Up close, he saw thin lines around the woman's face and mouth, lines that even her heavy makeup couldn't cover. Despite the trendy clothes, Jun guessed she was about the same age as his mother.

Chris spoke first. "Excuse me, are you Mrs. Dent?"

"You must be Jillian!" she said brightly. Her hazel eyes leapt from Chris's face to her disheveled hair. "Oh, we should get started right away," she said.

Mrs. Dent let her feet fall from the desk, catapulting herself out of the chair. Before Chris could say a word, Mrs. Dent seized her hand and towed her to the mirror covering the front wall. "So what's it going to be today?" she asked, kneading Chris hair.

"My name's not . . ."

"You prefer Jill? Not a problem. I'm Rebecca, but everybody calls me Becky." Mrs. Dent teased out a lock of Chris's hair, then held it up for examination in the mirror. "Now what do you think? Highlights?"

"Lady, if you come near me with a pair of scissors, I'll . . ."

"Uhhh . . ." Jun interrupted, "she's not Jillian."

"You're not Jillian?" she asked Chris's reflection.

"No," Chris said firmly.

"I guess we've got a case of mistaken identity here," Mrs. Dent said.

"There seems to be a lot of that going around," Jun muttered.

Chris shook loose from Mrs. Dent's grasp and positioned herself behind Jun. He thought that was funny given the difference in their height. Like a giraffe hiding behind a fire hydrant.

Mrs. Dent turned her eyes on Jun. They widened with recognition.

"Wait, I know you," she said. "You're the kid who broke through the firewall-thingie."

Jun sighed. "It's a filtering system."

"Didn't you get in trouble?"

"I'm here to clear my name," Jun said. "Do you mind if I ask you a few questions?"

Mrs. Dent strolled back to the reception desk. "Ask away. You can see how busy we are," she said, gesturing around the empty room. She fell back into the chair and continued to work on her nails. Each one, Jun noted, extended a half inch from her fingertips and was elaborately painted with swirls of purple and pink.

Mrs. Dent caught him staring. She held all ten fingers out for inspection. "You like them?"

Jun gave voice to the first answer that popped into his head.

"They must be hard to type with," he said.

A look passed between Mrs. Dent and Chris. "He doesn't have any sisters, does he?" the hairdresser asked.

"Only child," Chris confirmed.

Mrs. Dent nodded slowly as if this verified some long-held suspicion.

Not five minutes in the shop and already Jun had lost control of the conversation. He closed his eyes and recalled the police interrogations he'd seen on TV. Detectives always start with easy questions. Loosen up the witness.

"When do you volunteer at the middle school?"

"Mondays mornings. The shop's closed then, anyways."

"But you were there Friday afternoon."

"They call me in when the librarian is sick," she said. "Happens from time to time."

"You don't mind?"

"My daughter went to that school. It's my way of giving back."

"Did Mr. Hastings talk to you this morning about the pictures?"

"He did. And let me tell you, the man was not happy. He wanted to know exactly who was on this one computer between such-and-such times. So I told him it was you."

She said it so casually, like she was picking an item off a menu, instead of accusing him of a get-kicked-out-of-school crime.

"But you don't even know me," Jun said, incredulous.

"That's right, so I described you to a couple of the kids that were in the library at the time. I asked them if they knew an Asian boy with hair that sticks up in the back."

Jun resisted an urge to smooth down his spiky tufts.

"One of the kids knew you and gave me your name," Mrs. Dent continued, "but it was funny because I was like, 'June? It can't be June. It was a boy.'"

She was the third grownup that day to draw attention to his name. Jun shoved his frustration aside and focused instead on crafting his next question. The shape of his life over the next week depended on Mrs. Dent's answer. "Do you have a list of everyone who was in the library on Friday during block seven?"

Mrs. Dent met his eyes with an amused smile. "Honey, it's a library, not the hall of records."

Jun's shoulders slumped. "So there's no list?"

"At least forty kids move in and out of that place in an hour. We can't keep track of them all."

With no way of knowing who was in the library, Jun had no place to start. He might as well pick names at random out of the school directory. At that rate, he should have the whole thing wrapped up in a year or two.

"Did you see anyone else at that computer?" Jun asked.

"Not that I can remember."

"Was there anyone in the library that looked, you know, suspicious?"

"You mean someone in a hat and a trench coat?" Mrs. Dent said dramatically.

"Anyone who looked out of the ordinary?" he clarified.

Mrs. Dent shook her head, making her blond curls sway. "Sorry, kid. I got nothing."

The bell over the door jangled. An older woman with short white hair and round sunglasses stepped inside. Mrs. Dent straightened. "Jillian?" she called.

The woman smiled and waved.

"Yeah, she looks just like me," Chris whispered in Jun's ear.

Mrs. Dent got to her feet. "Well kids, I've got work to do."

Jun felt extra small standing next to Mrs. Dent in her three-inch heels. A note of desperation crept into his voice. "Are you sure there's nothing else you remember?"

Mrs. Dent looked like she was about to say no, then she paused and bit her bottom lip. There was a look of something half-remembered in her squinted eyes. "You know, there was this one kid. He wears one of those flash drive thingies around his neck, and he's always hanging around the library after school."

"He got a name?" Jun asked.

Mrs. Dent searched the ceiling tiles for the answer. After a moment, she said sheepishly, "I only know what the kids call him."

"What's that?"

"I probably shouldn't be repeating this," she said, then added in a whisper, "The kids call him Little D."

Jun thanked Mrs. Dent and headed outside, Chris following at his heels.

"Want to head back to the school?" Chris asked. "Little D might still be there."

"No," he said firmly.

Jun could count his good friends on one hand and still have a finger and a thumb left over. And today, between interviews with Mr. Dunne, Charlie Bruno, Mr. Hastings, Mr. Jolinski, and Mrs. Dent, Jun had had enough face time with new people to last him a month!

The real detective work would be done by computer. It was the twenty-first century, after all. Why bother wringing answers out of reluctant witnesses? Everything he needed to know waited for him on the internet.

He hurried home to research a kid named Little D.

Chapter 5

After dropping Chris off, Jun reviewed his day. He'd been slammed into the lockers by an overprotective boyfriend, accused of a cowardly crime he didn't commit, and teased by a hairdresser who looked forty, but dressed like she was eighteen. And his day wasn't over yet. He still had to smile at his parents and pretend nothing was wrong while he searched for the mysterious Little D.

Before opening the door, Jun considered explaining his predicament to his mother. It wouldn't hurt to have some adult help. He quickly dismissed the idea. His mother had a tendency to overreact. If she got involved, she'd contact his father, and the superintendent, and her lawyer, and probably the National Guard. She'd work so hard to protect him that Principal Hastings would have no time to track down the real cyberbully. With his mother on the case, Jun knew he'd never be expelled, but the true culprit would never be found either.

This had to be handled quietly, he decided. Under the radar.

He unlocked the front door and pushed inside, leaving his backpack and shoes beside the door. A set of official-looking documents caught his eye. They were fanned out on the console table next to the dish where he deposited his keys. Taking the documents in his hands, Jun realized they were recommendation forms, part of his application to Wellington. His mother had carefully filled out his name and contact information. According to the directions, the next step was for Jun to deliver the forms to his math and language arts teachers.

As if he didn't already have enough to do this week!

Wellington was a feeder school for MIT, the very same university his father had attended. Although his mother never said it out loud, Jun knew she longed to have him continue the family legacy. The parental pressure didn't really bother Jun, though. All the best video game designers had degrees from MIT.

And there was another advantage in it for Jun, too. His mother had assured him that the day he received his acceptance letter, she'd buy him the smartphone of his choice. And he needed one badly. His current phone was two years old. Practically prehistoric.

A gold post-it note clung to the bottom of the top form. On it, his mother had written: *Please have your teachers fill out these forms this week.*

Jun reread the directions. The deadline wasn't until Christmas. Two months away! He set the forms back on the table. They could wait for a week when he wasn't facing expulsion.

Heavy footsteps echoed from the staircase opposite the door. His mother's voice followed. "Jun, could you give me a hand with this?"

Jun jogged to the staircase and looked up. His mother's feet came into view first. There was something large, black, and rectangular in her hands. Jun bent at the waist to get the whole picture.

The screen from his computer was pressed against her stomach, her slender hands gripping the base. She had neglected to disconnect any of the cables, and now they dragged behind, their heavy metal plugs clattering down each step.

A lock of hair fell over her eyes. She puffed it aside. "I could use a hand here."

Jun dashed up the steps and seized the cables, lifting the thick power cords. "Why are you taking this out of my room?" he asked.

She gestured with her chin. "Grab that one too."

She carried his docking station in the crook of her arm. From it spilled the thin wire attached to the mouse. Transferring the other two cables into his left hand, he bent and scooped up the mouse, shaking it next to his ear to make sure nothing was broken.

Tethered together, they bumped down the remaining steps. His mother steered them to the living room, where they set everything down on a desk across from the TV.

Jun draped a protective arm over his monitor. "What's going on?"

His mother looked distracted. She started again to the stairs. "I'll get the laptop next."

Jun circled around her and put one hand on the banister, barring her way. "Not until you tell me what's happening." He wasn't usually so forward, especially with his mother, but this was his *computer*!

Mrs. Li wiped her brow. "I just spoke with Chris's mom. She said there was another incident of cyberbullying at school. Did you hear about that?"

Jun lowered his eyes. "A few people were talking about it." One of them happened to be the principal, but Jun decided to keep that tidbit to himself.

"Mrs. Pine told me the target this time was Kimmie Cole," his mother continued. "Do you know her?"

At the mention of Kimmie's name, two big hands gripped Jun's stomach and squeezed hard. "Um . . . no," he managed. "I mean, I've probably seen her around school, but we're not friends or anything."

"Well, I'm not taking any chances," Mrs. Li said decisively. "I've done some reading online, and the first suggestion on every website is to place the child's computer in the family room, so their online activities can be supervised."

There went his chance of finding Little D!

"Mo-om," Jun whined. "Is this really necessary? I mean . . . it's me." He opened his eyes wide. The innocent are always wide-eyed.

His mother tilted her head sympathetically. "I know, honey," she said gently. "Of course I don't think you'd bully anyone. This is for your protection. A parent supervising her child's online activities might be able to stop an attack before it starts."

That sounded like a direct quote from whatever paranoid website she'd been reading.

"But no one is bullying me, Mom," Jun said. He immediately thought about Charlie Bruno and his brief, violent encounter with the school lockers. The lump on the back of his head started to throb again.

His mother read his expression. "Something wrong?"

He hated lying, but what was the alternative? If she reacted like this to *rumors*, she'd completely flip when she discovered he was Mr. Hastings's prime suspect.

"Things are fine, Mom," Jun said. "Come on. Let's get

the rest of it."

His mother hesitated on the first step. "Are you sure?"

Jun would do anything, even give up his computer, to stop the conversation before she stumbled onto the land-mine that was the truth.

"Positive," he said.

His mother tousled his hair. "You're a good kid."

An aching knot, the size of a golf ball, formed in his throat. Good kids don't break through filtering systems. Good kids don't lie to their mothers.

"Oh, by the way," his mother said, starting up the stairs, "I just received an email from Wellington."

"Really?" he said, his spirits lifting. "What did it say?"

"Because of high demand this year, they've accelerated the timetable on their admissions process. Applications are now due by the end of October, which means you'll have to ask your teachers for a recommendation this week."

"This WEEK?" he half-shouted.

Jun's whole life was coming apart like wet cotton candy! His chances of being accepted to Wellington had just gone from excellent to astronomically slim.

"Are you alright?" his mother asked, pausing in her steps.

"It's just short notice," he explained. "But if I talk to my teachers tomorrow, I guess they can have the recommendations ready by Friday."

"Perfect," his mother said, continuing upstairs.

Jun followed slowly behind. If his teachers had heard the rumors floating around the school, there wasn't a single one of them who would write a recommendation for the school's newest cyberbully.

Chapter 6

Tuesday

After the final bell the next day, Jun waited for Chris outside her history class. She stood beside her desk, chatting with friends from her basketball team while the rest of the students filed out.

"Come on," Jun muttered, eager to begin his investigation.

Not that he knew much about investigating. Normally, he'd google whatever he wanted to know, and learn everything from the information avalanche that followed. But with his computer in the living room and his mother looking over his shoulder every two seconds, Jun was paranoid about conducting the search. Instead, he had turned to the only other resource in his house — the family library.

Books, as far as Jun was concerned, were like old

computers. They were slow, cumbersome, and their search engines (a.k.a. the table of contents) were horribly inefficient. Still, he considered it a stroke of good luck when he stumbled across a collection of old detective novels on the bottom shelf of a bookcase in the family room.

As he waited for Chris, book covers from the forties and fifties flashed through his mind. According to those novels, the average detective was a white male in his late thirties. He wore a hat, a buttoned-up trench coat, and a grim, tight-lipped expression, like the whole world was against him.

Jun could sympathize with that last part.

A trio of girls stood on the opposite side of the hallway. The one in the middle, a girl with short brown hair and thick-framed glasses, held her phone at arm's length. Two of her friends pressed close, angling for a better view. Jun didn't need to see the screen to know what they were looking at. Apparently, the Kimmie pictures hadn't lost any of their appeal overnight.

"Come on, Chris," Jun muttered again.

For every hour wasted, there could be fifty, maybe a hundred new people who'd view the pictures as word spread to the high school and the surrounding town. Mr. Jolinski had taken the incriminating pictures off the school's website immediately, but not before students had posted them to other sites. The IT director had tracked down those sites too, but the photos kept popping up in new locations, like stubborn weeds.

"Took you long enough," he said when Chris finally emerged from the classroom.

"And a big hello to you too."

"Let's go," Jun said, starting down the hall.

Chris jogged to catch up. "What's the rush?"

"We're going on a field trip."

"Where to?"

"The library," he said. "There's this goon down there. I want to run him over the coals and see if he sings."

Jun had decided that the best way to become a detective was to immerse himself in their language. He'd read the first chapters of three different novels to prepare.

Chris looked at him like he was speaking ancient Greek. "Uhh . . . you want to try that again?"

Jun spoke out of the left side of his mouth, as if the other side held a lit cigarette. "We need to grill a possible stool pigeon. Tighten the screws and get him to squeal."

Chris stopped him. "Listen, I'm going home right now if you don't start talking like a normal person."

Jun translated, "We need to talk to Dion Little and see what he knows about Kimmie."

"You could've just said that!" Chris said, continuing to her locker. "How'd you figure out Little D's real name?"

"Before lunch I talked to Kevin — he's an eighth grader

in the computer club. Kevin recognized the nickname right away. Two weeks back, he and Dion worked on a science lab together, and he confirmed what Mrs. Dent told us — Dion hangs out in the library most afternoons."

"Lots of people hang out in the library," Chris reminded him. "How will we find Dion?"

"Kevin said to look for an oversized pair of headphones."

Chris spun the dial on her combination lock. "Alright, I'll come with you. Somebody's got to watch your back."

Jun puffed out his chest. "I think I can handle a kid named Little D."

***

"That's Little D?" Jun said when they spotted the giant eighth grader in the school library.

From behind, Chris laid a hand on Jun's shoulder. "Aren't you glad I came?"

"Must be one of those reverse nicknames," Jun commented.

"You think?"

Dion sat with his back to them at a computer station near the windows. Though not as tall as Chris, he was nearly twice as wide. His arms, below the short sleeves of his white T-shirt, had a soft, doughy quality to them. His midsection bulged around the armrests of the computer chair. An extra-large pair of headphones stretched across the parallel lines of his cornrows. Dion bounced his head in time to the music.

Chris nudged Jun from behind. "Go on. See if you can get him to squeal."

Staring at Dion's mountainous back, Jun regretted the tough-guy talk in the hallway. He approached cautiously, almost tiptoeing. He quickly realized this made little sense. Dion probably couldn't hear much with those headphones on.

Jun stopped a few feet behind him. "Excuse me?"

Dion's head continued to bob. His fingers flew across the keyboard with a steady tapping sound like raindrops against a window.

Jun stepped closer. Now he could hear the muffled sounds of the pulsing music. "Dion?" he asked, louder.

The big kid wiggled his shoulders, responding not to Jun's voice, but to a change in the rhythm of the music.

Jun looked to Chris for advice. She reached out and tapped the air, then nodded her head at Dion. Jun followed her silent instructions and tapped him on the shoulder.

Dion jumped. "Aaah!"

Kicking his feet, he rolled his chair away from Jun and slammed into Chris, giving him another fright. "Aaaaah!" Dion slid his headphones to his shoulders. His other hand covered his chest. "What the heck are you doing? Trying to give me a heart attack?"

"Sorry," Jun said quickly. "I didn't mean to startle you."

"You didn't startle me," Dion said. "You scared the crap out of me."

"Sorry," he said again. "I was just trying to . . ."

Halfway through his apology, Dion scooted back to the computer and switched off the monitor. Jun realized too late that he should've noted what Dion was working on, or at least what program he'd been using. Before the screen went black, Jun did glimpse one name — Arthur Radley.

Jun needed to take charge of this situation. He needed to be a detective. He rolled his shoulders back and stood taller. Not that it helped much. Dion, sitting in his chair, was about the same height as Jun was standing.

"Are you Dion Little?"

Dion's eyes bounced from Jun to Chris then back again. "Who wants to know?"

"The name's Jun Li."

"Okay, but who's the skyscraper?" Dion said, indicating Chris with a jerk of his head.

"Oh, that's real funny, you . . ." Chris started.

Jun stepped in front of her. "This is Chris," he said. "And she's very friendly, right Chris?" Jun gave her a look that said *behave*. Dion was their only suspect. Beating the snot out of him wouldn't help their chances of extracting information.

Chris pinched her mouth closed. Glaring at Dion, she

sat down on the corner of a nearby desk. Jun felt for her. Chris sat whenever she felt self-conscious about her height.

Dion lifted his smartphone from the desk to check the time. "Hey, nice to meet you and all, but I really gotta get back to it."

Jun eyed the phone greedily. "Is that the Laser XL2?"

Dion held it up proudly. "You know it."

"But the XL2 came out just last week."

Dion shrugged. "I'm an early adopter."

"That phone is super expensive!"

"That's if you get the top-end model. This one here only has half the memory, but that's more than enough for me."

"Still, it must be at least four hundred dollars."

"Not if you shop around, Jun. Value Barn's got 'em for cheaper."

"For real?"

"Uh, Jun," Chris said, "could I talk to you a minute?" She waved him away from Dion and bent for a private conversation. "I thought you were going to . . . you know, run him over the coals?"

"I don't want to annoy him," Jun said, exasperated. "I mean, this guy probably eats sixth graders for breakfast."

"Forget that! The kid's a giant marshmallow," Chris said. "And I've got your back, so there's nothing to worry about." She spun him around and pushed him toward

Dion. "Go make him sing."

Jun, still unsure of himself, took small steps back to Dion. "Uh, I wanted to ask you a few questions about Kimmie Cole."

Dion's eyes narrowed. He nodded slowly, like he should've seen this coming. "Well, you can forget it. I ain't got nothin' to say."

Jun looked to Chris, wondering what he'd done wrong. He saw the same confusion mirrored on her face.

"You think you're the first ones to come asking about Kimmie?" Dion asked. "Just because I got computer skills, people think I'm out to get her." He shook his head. "You know, in elementary, I got good grades, and I shared my tater tots at lunch. Everyone thought I was the man, you know? Honor roll, citizenship awards, stuff like that. Now, just because I know how to push a mouse around, I get rounded up with the usual suspects."

"You're not the only one." Jun said, pleased to know that Mr. Hastings had spoken to *other* computer geeks.

"They got you too?"

"Yesterday morning."

Dion thumped the desk with his fist. "I don't even know the girl."

"That's what I said."

"Jun . . ." Chris said, disapproving.

Off track again. Some detective he was turning out to

be! He returned to his list of questions. "So Kimmie never came after you?"

"That's what nobody seems to understand. Why would I go after someone I don't even know?"

Jun couldn't argue with that logic. He'd used the same defense with Mr. Hastings. He tried another approach. "The librarian said you're here almost every day after school."

"What, hanging out in the library is against the rules?"

Chris folded her arms over her chest. "It depends on what you're doing."

"I'm updating Mr. Wainwright's website," Dion explained.

Jun knew the name. He was an English teacher in the eighth grade.

"He's got me posting all his homework assignments and stuff on the internet," Dion continued. "Only Mr. Wainwright's a real stiff, so when he says 'internet' he pronounces every syllable real slow, like this —" Dion puckered his lips. "*In-ter-net.*"

Jun tried to keep a straight face. It was hard not to like Dion.

"Is Mr. Wainwright paying you?" he asked.

"Nah, it's practice, you know? Still, it never hurts to have a teacher owe you a favor, especially when you're getting dragged into the principal's office. Know what I mean?"

Having already spent twenty minutes with Mr. Hastings, Jun needed no further explanation.

"And just so you know," Dion continued, "I was in Mr. Wainwright's class during block seven on Friday, so there's no way I could have posted those pictures. Ask Mr. W if you don't believe me."

"I will," Jun said.

"Now guys, I gotta get back to business. We done?"

Jun thanked Dion and exited the library with Chris trailing behind. As he walked down the hall, Jun kept looking back over his shoulder as if someone were following them.

Chris glanced back. "What is it?"

"I don't know . . . I think I missed something."

Chris waved her hand. "Forget it. Dion's just like you. He's got no reason to go after Kimmie."

"I know," Jun said, "but you saw how he reacted, turning off the monitor. He's hiding something."

"Did you see anything on the screen?"

"Not really."

Chris stopped him. "Is that a yes or a no?"

"It all happened so fast," Jun said. "I couldn't tell what program he was using, or even if he was on the internet. But I think I saw a name."

"Out with it!" she demanded.

"It was Arthur Radley. Does that name mean anything

to you?"

"No, but it's a clue, right?"

Jun shrugged. He had expected the clues he'd find along the way to be like flares, burning bright red in the night sky, clearly laying out a direction, the next step. This clue was more like a chirping cricket in the basement — impossible to track down.

Nevertheless, Jun filed the name away for later use.

Chapter 7

Wednesday

Jun found his English teacher, Mrs. Rabinowitz, alone in her classroom before lunch. He entered, holding his private school recommendation form behind his back.

Mrs. Rabinowitz stared intently at her laptop. The bluish glow of the screen reflected off the lenses of her fashionable pink-framed glasses.

Jun sucked in a deep breath and tried to summon his courage. He knew this wasn't going to work, but what choice did he have?

"Excuse me," he said.

"Jun!" she said, startled. "I didn't see you there."

Immediately, she began to organize the clutter on her desk. She stowed a pack of post-it notes in her top drawer, dropped two pens into a coffee mug, and tapped an uneven pile of essays against the desktop until they formed one neat stack. Jun wasn't surprised by her sudden burst of activity. Since the rumors started, few of his teachers would look him straight in the eyes.

"Umm . . ." Jun started, pulling the form from behind his back. "I have a favor to ask."

Her face flushed. "It's . . . uh, a little early for recommendation letters, isn't it?"

"Sorry, I wouldn't bother you unless it was important."

"The term ends next week," she said, "and I'm drowning in essays right now. Can it wait a week?"

Jun couldn't blame her for stalling. No sense writing a recommendation for a kid who might get expelled.

"Actually, no, it can't," he said. "I'm applying to Wellington."

"Really?" she said.

Her reaction told him that applying to the state's most prestigious private school was a bold move for a cyberbully.

"They've accelerated their timetable," Jun explained. "Applications are due by the end of the month. I know it's short notice, but I was hoping you could help me out."

Mrs. Rabinowitz looked down at her desk, then back up at Jun. She grimaced. "I want to. I'm just swamped with work right now. Maybe you could . . ." she scrunched up her face, wrinkling the bridge of her nose, "ask someone else?"

Jun tried not to let his disappointment show. "Um . . . sure."

He dragged himself away, wondering if there was anyone in the school who hadn't heard the rumors. Before he reached the door, Mrs. Rabinowitz called his name. He turned, and this time she met his gaze and held it. "I'm sorry I can't help."

"It's okay," he said, wondering if they were still talking about the recommendation letter.

Outside the classroom, he leaned his shoulder against the cold concrete. Wellington had always been his dream. But at this rate, not even McDonald's would accept an application from him.

"There you are!"

It was Chris, working her way against the flow of kids headed to the cafeteria.

"How'd it go with Mrs. Rabinowitz?" she asked.

"Not great."

"Well, this might cheer you up," Chris said. "I overheard something in the locker room."

Jun realized he had it backward. Before he could score a teacher recommendation letter, he had to clear his name. "Tell me," he said with fresh energy.

"Not here." She led him through the halls until she found an empty classroom.

"Why all the secrecy?" he asked. "Can't we talk in the

cafeteria?" He worried that a passerby might see a boy and a girl alone in the classroom and get the wrong idea.

"The caf's too noisy," Chris said. "I'd have to shout and someone might overhear."

Jun hadn't seen Chris this serious since last year's play-offs. "What's going on?"

Chris parked herself on a nearby desk. "So I was getting dressed, right? And I overhead this girl on my basketball team talking about how Kimmie got exactly what she deserved."

The empty classroom, combined with Chris's urgent tone, had raised Jun's hopes for a juicy clue. The actual information was a disappointment.

"Lots of kids feel that way," he said.

"Yeah, but this was Leah Armstrong."

"So?"

"Leah used to be friends with Kimmie Cole."

"Used to be?" Jun echoed, suddenly curious.

"That's right. Past tense."

Jun took a step closer. "When did they stop hanging out?"

"Do I look like I keep her social calendar?"

"Can you guesstimate?"

"I don't know." Chris shrugged. "Sometime in September."

Jun's spirits lifted. A new suspect! What had caused Kimmie and Leah's friendship to end? He would have to find out. Today, if possible.

"Do you know where Leah lives?" he asked.

"Yeah, the Hornets had dinner at her house once before a game." Chris's eyebrows rose. "You planning another field trip?"

Before he could answer, the sound of footsteps reached his ears. Jun turned to see a large girl filling the doorway. He recognized her right away. It wasn't so much her face that triggered his memory. It was her stomach. The very same stomach Kimmie had posted pictures of online.

Rachel Cook's hands gripped the sides of the doorway. Behind her, two friends waited in the hall.

"What's going on in here?" Rachel asked, her eyes bouncing between Chris and Jun.

Jun knew what she was implying. "Nothing," he said, taking a step back from Chris. "We're just talking."

"Oh, that's right," Rachel said, nodding her head. "You're busy these days trying to help Kimmie Cole."

If he denied it, he was a liar. If he said yes, he was helping the girl who'd posted the humiliating pictures of Rachel. Either way, it was trouble.

"This is a private conversation," he said evasively.

Rachel invited herself into the classroom. "Call me crazy," she continued, "but I kinda like school better when Kimmie's not around."

"I'm not sure you understand . . ."

"No, I get it. Nobody cares when a fat girl like me gets picked on. But when Princess Kimmie's attacked, everyone rushes in to help."

Rachel's proclamations about her size left Jun feeling awkward and tongue-tied. Maybe that was the whole idea.

Rachel continued, "Do you guys realize you're tracking down the kid who went after the meanest girl in school? If you ask me, and nobody did, you should give that person a medal."

"Shouldn't you be at lunch?" Chris asked.

Rachel rolled her eyes. "You think just 'cause I'm fat I can't miss a few minutes of lunch?" She looked over her shoulder. "You believe this, girls?"

Rachel's friends wagged their heads.

"Look, I'm not telling you what to do," she continued, "but if it were me, I wouldn't be working too hard to help Kimmie, if you know what I mean."

"Yeah, Rachel," Chris said, "we get it. Now *get out.*"

Rachel turned to her. "Kimmie's bad news. She's the plague. She infects everyone around her."

"Wow, tell us how you really feel," Chris said flatly.

Rachel was about to reply, and judging by her curled upper lip, it was going to be something nasty. "How come Kimmie went after you?" Jun asked, hoping to distract her.

Rachel whirled around. "'Cause I caught Little Miss Perfect doing something she's not supposed to do," she said. "Those pictures had it right. Kimmie eats a big lunch and then stuffs her finger down her throat for dessert."

"You saw her?" Chris asked.

"Caught her in the girls' bathroom back in May. I told her I wouldn't say anything. And then that picture of me shows up on the internet." Rachel's lips twisted. She looked like she was about to spit. "Kimmie's way of making sure I stay quiet. She said that if I breathed one word about what I saw, she'd publish the *other* pictures she took in the locker room."

Jun fixed Rachel with his most confident stare. At least, he hoped it looked confident. He was new at this whole detective thing.

"Where were you on Friday during block seven?"

Rachel smiled knowingly. "Ha! You think I did this. I wish."

"So where were you?" he pressed.

"Ask Chris. She knows." Rachel backed into the hall-way. A moment later, she poked her head back into the classroom. "Oh by the way, next time you lovebirds might want to pick a less obvious spot to make out."

Jun let that jab slip past him. It was only about the millionth time he'd been teased for having Chris as a best friend. Chris had the opposite reaction. She marched to the doorway and shouted after Rachel, "We are not LOVE-BIRDS!"

Jun laid a hand on her arm. "I don't think the kids in the sixth-grade wing heard you."

"It's not funny, Jun."

"She only says those things because she knows it makes you mad."

"I am *not* mad," Chris growled, red-faced.

Jun attempted to redirect Chris's thoughts before her head exploded. "So where was Rachel on Friday, during block seven?"

"She's got math with me," she said, clearly annoyed at being the one to provide Rachel's alibi.

"So she couldn't have posted the pictures?"

Chris folded her arms across her chest and turned her chin to the windows. "She was in class the whole time."

Jun stepped out into the hall and watched Rachel disappear down the end of the long hallway. Her words banged around inside his head. "She's not right, is she?" he asked.

Chris joined him in the hall. "About what?"

"About Kimmie. Is the school really better off without her?"

"Don't listen to her," Chris said. "Rachel's just watching out for herself."

Jun nodded, but the idea sat like a brick in his stomach. Once the cyberbully had been caught, Kimmie would return to school. But what if Kimmie, after this was all over, went back to terrorizing kids on the internet? By clearing his name, would Jun be unleashing the Kimmie Virus back on the school? Or would Kimmie, a cyberbully herself, change her ways after getting a taste of her own medicine? Not liking any of the answers, Jun chose not to think about it any further.

✳ ✳ ✳

Wednesday was an early release day. School dismissed at one o'clock for teacher professional development. Jun was grateful for the head start and left directly for Leah Armstrong's house with Chris.

As he walked along the sidewalk, Jun pulled a bag of cheese balls from his jacket pocket. He opened the bag close to his nose so he could catch the first puff of cheesy goodness wafting out. He popped one ball into his mouth. Chris glared her disapproval.

"What?" Jun asked.

"How can you eat those things?" she asked, as if eating cheese balls was as bad as shooting endangered animals.

"It's easy. You just put one in your mouth and chew."

"They're loaded with trans fat and artificial coloring."

Jun popped another in his mouth and crunched extra loud to show his defiance. "That's what makes them so good."

"You are what you eat," Chris muttered under her breath.

Jun shot her a quizzical look. "Did you just call me a cheese ball?"

Chris shrugged. "Look at your fingers and you tell me." A thick layer of orange cheese powder coated three fingers on his right hand. Jun licked each one clean. "That's the best part."

"You're just like Kimmie, you know," Chris said.

Jun did a double take. "Whaddaya mean?"

"You heard me."

"I have an eating disorder?"

"Every time you get a little jittery, you stick something in your mouth. Popcorn, chips, candy. Does that sound normal to you?"

Jun had never thought about it. His unexpected hunger attacks were like an itch. To make it go away, he just had to scratch. What was so wrong with that?

"It's not like I'm putting on weight." Jun raised his arms to show off his slender frame.

"Kimmie's not putting on weight either. That doesn't make it healthy."

He and Kimmie were nothing alike. His throat was a one-way street. Food went down and rarely came back up. Still, it wasn't worth arguing about. Food and exercise were two topics Chris was *always* right about. Even when she wasn't.

They walked another block, the sounds of their

footsteps punctuated every so often by the crunching of cheese balls. Before crossing the street, Chris stopped and frowned. She looked left and right.

"I thought you knew where she lived," Jun said.

"Just give me a minute."

Jun pointed one orange finger. "The sun sets in that direction. That's west."

"If I needed a boy scout, I'd call my little brother."

Ouch! That was harsh! "Everything alright?" he asked.

Chris found her bearings and turned left. "Listen, I'll do the all talking with Leah, okay?"

Jun jogged to catch up. "Why you?"

"Because it's *Leah Armstrong* we're talking to."

"So?"

"Ashley Eastman and Koko Jones will probably be there, too," she said, as if that explained everything.

The names meant nothing to Jun. "So?" he said again.

"Don't you ever look up from your school books?" Chris said. "Popular people are like a different species, Jun. You can't talk to them like normal people. If it weren't for my basketball connections, we wouldn't even get through the door."

"But if you're asking the questions," Jun said, "what am I going to do?"

"I don't know. Stand there and look pretty?"

Jun clamped a hand over his head to stamp down the

spiky hairs. They rebounded with astonishing stubbornness. "Any better?"

"You'll be beating the girls off with a stick," Chris said. "Now what should I ask?"

"We need to know what caused Kimmie and Leah to end their friendship. We know that Kimmie's weight problem is a source of embarrassment for her. Maybe Leah found out about Kimmie's weight issues and threatened to expose them. Kimmie then retaliated, leading Leah to strike back with the pictures."

"Why would Leah threaten to expose the secrets of her best friend?"

Jun frowned. "I don't know."

"And what did Kimmie do to retaliate? It had to be pretty awful to cause Leah to post those pictures."

"I don't know that either."

"Lots of holes in your theory," Chris said.

"Hey, I'm new to this sort of thing," he replied. "I didn't ask for this assignment. I was just in the wrong place at the wrong time."

"Doing the wrong thing," she reminded him.

Her words reverberated inside his head like a church bell. She was right. The filtering system was there for a reason — to keep students off restricted websites. If he hadn't been so obsessed about getting a perfect grade (better than perfect, really), he wouldn't have been on that computer

Friday and he wouldn't be in this situation right now.

"Relax," Chris said. "We'll figure this thing out before Mr. Hastings kicks you out of school."

Chris was trying to make him feel better. The key word there was *trying*. He was well aware of the stakes, but to hear them spoken out loud made his knees feel wobbly.

He said, "You forgot the part where Kimmie's boyfriend, Charlie, tries to use my face as a punching bag."

"It won't come to that."

"No, of course not," he said, but he didn't believe it.

And judging by the way Chris bit her bottom lip, neither did she.

Chapter 8

The front door was made of heavy, dark wood. A lion-headed knocker snarled down at them. Chris opted for the door bell instead.

Leah's mother answered the door. She was a petite woman in shorts and a tank top. A white towel lay over her shoulder. Her bare feet sported two sets of perfectly painted red toenails.

She took in the sight of the two strangers and then rested her shoulder against the door. "Can I help you?" she asked.

"We're here to see Leah," Chris said.

Mrs. Armstrong looked her up and down. "I know you, don't I?"

"You might. I play on Leah's team."

"You're the center."

A smile split Chris's face. It wasn't like people in the streets were running up every day to get autographs signed. "That's right."

"You scored twelve points in the game against Walpole."

Chris was nodding now. "Yep, that's me."

Mrs. Armstrong frowned. "You need to work on your foul shots, dear. You can't always rely on your height to get the ball through the hoop."

"O-okay, I'll remember that."

"Um . . . hi." Jun hoped to steer the conversation back on track. "I'm Jun, and we wanted to ask . . ."

"Jun? That's an interesting name. Is it Japanese?"

Jun was so accustomed to correcting people that he stuttered, "H-h-how'd you know?"

"I spent a semester in Tokyo. Part of a travel abroad program in college."

Jun had never been to Japan. But this woman with the last name *Armstrong* had? What was wrong with this picture?

"We were hoping to talk to Leah," Chris cut in. "I had a computer question that only she can answer."

"Then you've come to the right place," Mrs. Armstrong said, opening the door wide. "My Leah knows everything about computers."

Mrs. Armstrong led them down three steps into the

living room. While they waited on the oriental rug, she strode to the foot of the double-wide staircase and called for Leah. Jun took in the leather couch, the glass figurine case, and the expensive vases perched on the end tables, but his eyes were drawn to the entertainment center. DVR, DVD, Blu-ray, two video-game systems, and a Bose sound system sat in a polished wooden cabinet beneath the biggest flat screen TV Jun had ever seen.

Chris nudged him. "You're drooling," she whispered.

Jun snapped his mouth shut and focused his attention on Mrs. Armstrong. There was no response to her first call for Leah. She tried again, louder this time. When there was no answer a second time, she yelled, "LE-AH!" Her voice was surprisingly loud for such a small woman.

An upstairs door opened. Leah trotted onto the landing and leaned over the banister. "What?" she shot back. Noticing her mother wasn't alone, she smiled and said, "Oh, hey Chris."

Leah was built like a basketball player, tall with wide shoulders and long arms. She had a squarish, sturdy appearance. Jun knew some families where the daughter was almost a virtual clone of the mother. Not the case here.

"You've got company, Leah. Please come down and greet your guests." Mrs. Armstrong turned to Jun and Chris. "Nice to meet you." She started off, then paused and turned. "Oh, and Chris, remember . . ." She motioned a free throw.

"Right," Chris said, trying to hold onto her smile. "Got it."

Mrs. Armstrong nodded and padded off to a side room where Jun could see a blue yoga mat spread out on the floor.

Leah descended the staircase, stopping one step short of the bottom. This put her at eye level with Chris. "Sorry about that," she said. "My mother is the leading expert on just about everything." Her eyes darted from Chris to Jun and then back again. "So . . . um, what are you guys doing here?"

The uncertainty in Leah's voice told Jun that just because Chris played on her team didn't mean she expected her to show up one random afternoon.

"I wanted to talk to you about Kimmie Cole," Chris said.

Leah folded her arms over her chest and looked away.

"My least favorite topic."

"Are Koko and Ashley here?"

"Yeah, why?"

"We wanted to talk to them too," Chris said.

"Who's we?"

Chris introduced Jun.

Leah's face lit up like a Christmas tree. "You're the one who outed Kimmie!"

Given Leah's reaction, standing up to Kimmie was nothing short of a heroic act, on par with rescuing an infant from a burning building. Jun wished he could revel in that look of admiration for a few moments longer, but he had to set the record straight. "I'm the one accused of posting those pictures. We're here to find out who the real culprit is."

Leah blinked twice. "You think it's one of us?" She glared at Chris.

Chris waved a dismissive hand. "It's no big deal, really. We're just trying to cross people off our list."

"Actually," Jun said, "we must consider everyone a suspect until such time as they are proven . . ."

Chris slid in front of him. It was like the sun eclipsing the moon. "Ignore him. He's so low to the ground sometimes he doesn't hear things right. Seriously, this won't take more than five minutes. We just want to double-check our facts."

Leah bit her bottom lip, thinking it over. "Let me tell the others you're here." She dashed back up the staircase, her long legs taking the steps two at a time. Chris and Jun followed more slowly behind.

"I told you to be quiet," Chris hissed.

Jun had not planned on saying a word, but once he slipped into detective mode, keeping his mouth shut was as hard as walking up a water slide.

"You scared her," Chris continued. "She's probably up there right now with the other two, figuring out what lies they're going to tell us."

"Sorry," Jun said, unable to meet her eyes.

"Just let me do the talking, okay? I speak their language."

He shot her a sideways glance. "What language is that?"

"Girl," she said, striding ahead.

Jun followed Chris to the open door. She went in, but Jun hesitated. Inside, a purple scarf lay over a lamp providing the room's only light. It was enough to see the pink walls and stuffed bunny collection assembled on the puffy white bedspread. Even from the doorway, Jun could smell the heavily perfumed air.

Chris was right. The world of girls was completely alien to him. He didn't have a sister, and Chris didn't exactly qualify as girly. He'd have to follow her lead. He reluctantly stepped over the threshold.

A rectangular picture collage hung beside the door. Crisscrossing ribbon held a dozen photos in place. Jun scanned the pictures. Kimmie Cole's smiling face stared back at him from one of the pictures. If Leah and Kimmie were no longer friends, why display this picture? Had Leah simply forgotten to take it down, or was there something more going on?

A laptop sat atop a desk surrounded by three chairs.

Two of them were occupied by Koko and Ashley. Leah introduced the girls before dropping down onto the corner of the bed. Koko, a small Asian girl, had her black hair streaked blond. The darker-skinned Ashley had curly brown hair and a T-shirt that read: *Up to No Good.*

Signs didn't come more obvious than that, Jun thought.

"This is Chris," Leah said. "She's on my team."

To Ashley, Chris said, "Love your T-shirt."

Jun assumed that was Girl for hello.

"And this . . ." Leah gestured to him, "is her friend Jun."

Jun remained by the door and waved from his hip, determined to keep his vow of silence.

"So guys," Chris said, "I hate to get all serious on you, but the principal thinks Jun posted the pictures about Kimmie. If we don't figure out who's really behind it, Mr. Hastings might boot him out of school."

Leah shrugged. "Just tell us what you want to know."

"Okay," Chris said, pausing to gather her thoughts. "I'm guessing everyone here has seen the pictures."

"Only like fifteen times," Ashley said.

Leah nodded. "Kimmie got exactly what she deserved."

"Yeah," Koko agreed, "She had it coming."

Chris and Jun exchanged a knowing glance. This was confirmation of what Chris had overheard in the locker room. Still, Jun was not ready to move Leah to the top of the suspect list. The real bully, he decided, would play it cool when asked about the online attack. These girls were practically turning cartwheels.

"I thought you guys were, like, friends," Chris said to Leah.

"Not anymore," she replied. "We stopped hanging out a while back."

"What happened?"

Leah rolled her eyes and sighed. "It's so not worth talking about."

"Yeah, not worth talking about," Koko echoed.

"We came all the way over here, Leah," Chris said.

"Wow, you walked a whole half mile?" Leah replied.

"You must be some athlete," Koko said.

Koko was nothing more than a parrot, Jun realized. Chris wisely ignored her and fixed her eyes on Leah.

"Look, we need your help, okay?" Chris said.

Leah's lips were pressed together tightly as if she were holding something back.

"Come on," Chris said. "Hornets stick together, right?" Invoking the name of the team mascot seemed to do the trick. Leah wet her lips, then said slowly, "Okay, so this was, like, a month ago. I'd just gotten back from the game against Dedham."

"You were awesome in that game, by the way," Chris said, greasing the wheels.

"I know, right?" Leah said, sitting up straighter. "Anyway, I was super-tired afterward, but like an idiot I decided to hang out with the girls at Kimmie's house. Of course, I'm there only a half hour before I pass out on Kimmie's bed. So Kimmie, she takes her lipstick and she writes the words 'Feed Me' across my forehead." Her voice tightened. "Then she takes a picture of me and tapes it to a dozen lockers around the school."

"Why would Kimmie do something like that?" Chris asked.

Ashley answered first. "Because she's evil."

"Yeah," Koko agreed. "Totally evil."

Leah smiled bitterly and shook her head. "Not exactly."

Ashley's upper lip curled. "Why are you sticking up for her?"

"I'm not!" Leah said. She turned to Chris and Jun to explain. "For like a year now, Kimmie has been obsessed with telling the truth. If it's on her mind, she says it or posts it online. At first, it was kind of cool. Kimmie was fearless. She'd say anything. And then, it was like, she went too far. There's a line, you know, that sometimes you shouldn't cross? Kimmie would do more than cross that line. She'd leap over it and say things that were so hurtful. And the most bizarre part is, after it was all over, she'd turn around and pat herself on the back. Like, thank God she had the guts to say what everyone else was thinking."

"But Kimmie was your best friend," Chris pointed out. "Why would she write something so mean on your forehead?"

"Because of what happened at the mall," Ashley answered.

"Zip it, Ashley," Koko hissed.

"What? I can't talk about the mall?"

"It's private," Koko muttered under her breath.

"It's okay, Koko," Leah said, "Everybody already knows. What's two more?" Leah turned back to Chris and Jun. "A week before that, we were trying on clothes and Kimmie found these jeans she wanted to marry and she was all like, 'oh I hope they're not too big,' because she was crazy skinny and that was the smallest size they had. But she wouldn't shut up about it and I knew she was rubbing my face in it, because I'm . . ." she paused, fumbling for the right words. "I'm not built like her. Anyway, Kimmie was all like, 'I don't know why they don't make clothes in smaller sizes,' which was ridiculous because the ones she had were like doll clothes. So I was like, 'They'd fit better, if you weren't always sticking your finger down your throat.'"

Leah's words, once released, hung in the air, smothering any further conversation. Jun watched her. Her left eye twitched at the memory.

Chris was the first to break the silence. "Did you know for a fact that she was bulimic?"

"We suspected, but never actually saw her," Ashley said. "It was that fat blob Rachel Cook that caught her in the act. Kimmie was puking up her lunch in the girls' bathroom."

"That's why Kimmie posted that picture of Rachel," Jun interjected. "To keep her quiet."

Leah did a double take, as if remembering Jun was in the room. "I did the posting. Kimmie didn't want the pictures being traced back to her, so she asked the master for help." Leah laid a hand on her chest.

"Leah's totally the master," Koko said.

"And you had no problem helping her out?" Jun asked.

Ashley came to Leah's defense. "Why would she have a problem?" she snapped. "Rachel Cook isn't exactly the nicest girl in school."

"Take it easy, Ash," Chris said. "He was just asking."

"It was mean, I know," Leah conceded, "but let's face it, Rachel can't keep her mouth shut about her own weight, so you think she's going to pass up an opportunity to badmouth Kimmie? Plus, you should've seen the *other* pictures Kimmie took of Rachel. Trust me, we did that girl a favor."

Rachel Cook probably didn't see it that way, Jun thought.

"I don't get it," Chris said to Leah. "After those pictures were posted, how come you and Rachel didn't go after Kimmie?'

Leah shook her head. "You don't know Kimmie."

The way she was talking, Jun pictured Kimmie as a grizzly bear or some hulking serial killer, not a girl who couldn't weigh more than eighty pounds.

"If I went after Kimmie," Leah said, "she'd make it her personal mission to tell the whole world every dirty secret she knows about me. Kimmie and I have been friends since third grade, so she knows a *lot*."

Chris finally got around to the question that Jun would've started with. "Where were you during block seven on Friday?"

"Same place as always. Science with Mr. Gruber."

"I'm in that class, too," Koko added.

"I've got math with Mrs. Washington," Ashley said.

"Well, I guess that's it," Chris said, looking to Jun for confirmation.

A dozen unanswered questions lined up inside Jun's head, demanding to be asked. He could feel the weight of them pushing at the back of his throat.

"Who else knew about Kimmie's bulimia?" he blurted out.

"Jun . . ." Chris warned.

He ignored her. "Someone else must have known her secret."

Ashley stood up. "What's it to you?"

"The person who exposed her secret had to be someone

close to Kimmie," Jun said, "or else they wouldn't know about her eating disorder."

"What are you saying?" Ashley took a step toward Jun. "Are you saying it was one of us?"

Ashley was trying to intimidate him. And it was working.

"I . . . uh . . ."

"You know," Chris cut in, "I think we have everything we need. We'll be going now, right Jun?"

Jun huddled close. "I've got more questions, Chris," he whispered.

"You're done. Trust me." She herded him to the door.

Backing out of the room, the same picture from the collage caught his eye. In it, Leah and Kimmie stood on either side of a pretty girl with blond hair. Deep dimples on the blond's face dotted the ends of her closed-lipped smile. All three girls wore field hockey uniforms and leaned against the trunk of a silver convertible. Jun didn't recognize the middle girl, but it was obvious that Leah and Kimmie knew her, given the way their arms hung around her shoulders. Jun plucked the picture from the collage and sidestepped Chris.

"Who's this?" he asked, his finger tapping the middle girl.

A look rocketed between the three girls. Jun was no expert on interpreting facial expressions, especially ones from girls, but if he had to guess, he'd say the rough translation was something like, *Oh crap!*

"God, is that still up?" Leah said. "I meant to throw that out months ago."

"Didn't she move away?" Ashley asked.

Jun asked, "Does she have a name?"

"It's Melanie something," Leah said.

"Does she go to Brookfield?"

"She used to," Ashley said. "She transferred schools at the end of last year. Not that it's any of your business."

Jun directed his next question at Leah. "Was she friends with Kimmie?"

"Not really."

"They look pretty friendly in the picture," he said.

"That's middle school," Leah replied. "Friends one day, enemies the next."

Jun pounced. "So she's Kimmie's enemy?"

Leah shook her head. "She isn't anything anymore. Not to me or Kimmie."

"Or me," Koko added, folding her arms with finality.

Jun took in all three girls. He wanted to press on, but he suspected that he was already knee-deep in lies and half-truths. And he didn't want to cause any more trouble for Chris. She still had to practice with Leah. And from now on, more than a few passes might be aimed at Chris's head.

"Do you mind?" Jun held up his phone to take a

picture of the picture.

"You can keep it," Leah said. "If it's got Kimmie in it, I don't want it anymore."

Jun preferred a digital copy. He captured the shot and then returned the photo to the collage. Meanwhile, Chris said her goodbye to the girls. She was extra nice — trying to repair the damage he'd done, Jun guessed.

As they walked down the stairs, Chris said, "That's what you call being quiet?"

"What was I supposed to do? Leah said no one else knew about Kimmie's bulimia, then I saw the picture with Kimmie and Melanie looking all buddy-buddy. I had to ask."

Chris snatched the phone from his hand and stared at the frozen image on the display. "So how does dimple-girl figure into all this?"

"I don't know. But you saw how her friends reacted."

"Hard to miss."

Jun skipped down the staircase, his feet light on the steps. After three days of stumbling around in the dark, he'd finally hit on something important. Leah and the others obviously didn't want Jun to know about Melanie. Was it because she was the cyberbully?

Jun needed to learn everything there was to know about Melanie.

Her last name would be a good place to start.

Chapter 9

Jun dragged a straight-backed chair from the dining room and positioned it in front of the "living room" computer. The thinly padded cushion offered little comfort. Something about the space felt wrong, too. Working in his bedroom, he could shut the door. His room was small and cramped and wonderfully private. Here he was too exposed — which, if you asked his mother, was exactly the point.

He leaned the chair onto its back legs for a clear view into the kitchen. His mother was on her knees wiping down the refrigerator. Like everything else in the kitchen, it was already spotless. Scouring the appliances was part of her nighttime routine. The stovetop would get the treatment next, followed by the dishwasher.

Jun figured he had fifteen minutes.

Dropping the chair back onto all fours, he thumbed through a copy of Brookfield's student directory. It was mid-October, and the directory for the new school year had yet to be mailed home, which meant he had to use last year's copy.

Just as well, Jun thought. Melanie wouldn't be in the new directory.

Students were arranged alphabetically by last name. As he scanned down the list, Jun's index finger stopped under Kimmie Cole's name. He entered her phone number and address into his phone. Like it or not, he was working to help Kimmie, so he'd probably have to talk with her sooner or later. Jun hoped for later.

Jun had to scan nearly the entire list of seventh graders — all four hundred and thirty-five of them — to find Melanie's last name. He found her deep in the S section. Her last name was Stevens.

Jun shook the mouse to wake the sleeping computer and typed Melanie Stevens into Google, then added "Brookfield, MA" to narrow the search. The very first listing was a hit. So was the second, and the third, and the fourth. As far as Jun could tell, Melanie Stevens from Brookfield didn't just have a presence on the web. She'd built a shrine to herself online.

The highlights: at age four Melanie appeared in a

magazine ad for kids' toothpaste. At age eight, she created her own web page called *I Woof You* devoted to her golden retriever. Jun studied the small, twirling hearts that surrounded the title and wondered if Melanie had animated that particular graphic herself. At age thirteen, Melanie found Twitter. Making good use of all 140 characters, Melanie's entries were colorful, almost poetic, focusing mainly on her field hockey team's trip to the playoffs last year. They lost in the semifinals. Melanie had scored the team's only goal. Kimmie got the assist.

And that was it. No vicious blogs, no compromising pictures — nothing that would connect Kimmie to Melanie except for a few pictures of them playing field hockey together.

The floorboards behind him creaked. Jun's hand lashed out, seizing the mouse and quickly minimizing the screen.

"You're jumpy tonight," his mother said.

"You startled me," he said, praying his mother hadn't seen Melanie's picture on the screen. There was nothing about the blond field-hockey player that looked like homework.

"Did you get those recommendation forms to Mrs. Rabinowitz and Mr. Samuels?"

Mr. Samuels's response had been the same as Mrs. Rabinowitz's. Grades were due. No time to write a proper letter.

"Um . . . yes, I did," he lied.

"And will the letters be ready by Friday?"

Jun stared down at the keyboard. "Both teachers said they'd get right on it."

Mrs. Li nodded her approval. "Sounds like we're right on track."

Jun wasn't much of a liar. Yet here, in the space of a minute, he'd lied twice to his mother. He pushed the chair back from the desk. He needed to get out of the living room before more lies leaked from his mouth. "Um . . . I've got some homework I need to finish," he said, then added, "Upstairs."

Jun slid past his mother and crossed to the staircase. He had one foot on the first step when his mother called, "So what's her name?"

Apparently, he hadn't been fast enough with the mouse.

Jun tried to play dumb. "Who?"

Mrs. Li gestured to the computer. "The girl."

"Oh, her? She's . . . um . . . nobody."

"And does Ms. Nobody have a name?"

"Umm . . . it's Melanie."

"Melanie," his mother repeated slowly.

Jun knew he was on the verge of a second round of questions he couldn't answer. "I really should get going on my homework," he said, sprinting up the steps.

Homework took hours. Jun's mind simply wouldn't

focus. After ten, he crawled into bed, but couldn't sleep. One by one, the suspects paraded through his head. First there was Melanie Stevens. After a thorough internet search, he had found no incriminating link to Kimmie Cole. Maybe Melanie wasn't the cyberbully after all. Maybe she was just some random girl unfortunate enough to have Kimmie as a best friend. Then there was Dion Little. Jun still felt like he'd missed something during their talk. But, he reminded himself, the eighth grader had an alibi. He was in Mr. Wainwright's room during block seven — a fact, Jun realized, he still needed to verify. Thinking of Dion brought him logically to the name he'd seen on Dion's computer screen. Maybe the faceless Arthur Radley was the key to this whole mess.

His mind buzzed for another hour before he drifted into a light slumber. Around midnight, a realization made his eyelids snap open.

Melanie's last Twitter message was dated June 10th! In the four months since she left Brookfield, she hadn't posted a single byte of new information.

It was like Melanie Stevens had dropped off the face of the world wide web.

Chapter 10

Thursday

"So she just disappeared?" Chris asked.

"Digitally speaking, yes."

It was lunchtime and Chris had agreed to accompany Jun to the office.

"Jun, she didn't just vanish. She has to be somewhere."

"Agreed. So I crept downstairs after midnight and continued my search. After an hour, I still had nothing. I couldn't even figure out where she's going to school. That's why I want to talk to Mr. Hastings," Jun said, pulling open the office door. "He must know where she transferred."

They stopped at the receptionist's desk. "We're here to see Mr. Hastings," Jun said.

"He's got a meeting with the superintendent," Mrs. Kwon replied softly. "He won't be back until two. You might want to try again after school." The receptionist stood with a stack of papers pressed to her chest and walked to the end of the hall. She disappeared into an adjacent room where Jun heard the distinctive *chum-chump, chum-chump* of a copy machine.

"Well, look who it is," a voice said from behind.

Jun turned to find Rachel Cook parked on a bench outside the vice principal's office. The thin blue carpet beneath the bench had been worn through, probably by anxious kids shuffling their feet while waiting to see the V.P.

"Are you in trouble?" Jun asked.

"No," Rachel snapped. "I'm here to talk to Mr. Cooper. Someone called me 'fatty' during gym."

The familiar awkwardness Jun felt around Rachel gripped him once more.

"So what are you two doing here?" Rachel asked. "Still working for Kimmie?"

"Mind your own business, Rachel," Chris said.

"Kimmie *is* my business. She's everybody's business." Rachel shook her head. "Haven't kids been telling you about her? About what a wrecking ball she is? And you're still trying to help her?"

"It's not what you think." Jun met her eyes, then looked away. "Mr. Hastings thinks I posted those pictures. If I don't track down the real bully, he'll kick me out of school."

"He thinks you're behind this? You?" Rachel laughed.

"I heard the rumors, sure, but I thought — no way that's true!"

Chris had had the same reaction. Neither girl thought he was capable of such a malicious act. It was a compliment. Jun was sure of it. So why did he feel like he'd just been insulted?

"I mean, I could hack into the school's website if I wanted to," he said. "But I'd never do something like that."

"Then why are you here?"

"Well . . ." Jun started, unsure of why he was answering *her* questions. Wasn't he supposed to be the detective? "I'm kinda stuck right now."

"Oh, that's *too* bad." Rachel's voice dripped with false sympathy.

It occurred to Jun that Mr. Hastings might not be the only one with information about Melanie Stevens. Rachel had been in the seventh grade with Melanie. Sure, Brookfield was a big school, but maybe she knew something. It was worth a shot. Even the smallest bit of information would practically double what he currently knew. "Did you know a girl by the name of Melanie Stevens last year?"

"No."

Her answer came a little too quickly. "Are you sure?"

"Melanie Stevens . . ." Rachel looked at the ceiling and tapped her chin, making a big show of thinking it over. "Sorry. Never heard of her."

"You went to school with her last year," Jun said. "You must know *something*."

"What if I do?" Rachel asked. "Why would I do anything to help Kimmie?"

It was a good question. After a few seconds of thought, Jun shared the only answer that made sense. "Because it's the right thing to do."

"Was it right for Kimmie to post those pictures of me?" Rachel argued.

Jun said nothing.

"And what about Leah? She got it pretty bad too."

Mr. Hastings had given him this assignment. He was working for the principal. But there was no getting around it — to the rest of the world, it looked like he was taking orders from Kimmie Cole.

He changed the subject. "I did an internet search on Leah Armstrong. I couldn't find the *Feed Me* picture."

"That's because Kimmie didn't post it online, dummy. She printed it out and hung it up on two dozen lockers around school."

Jun mulled that over. "Why not post it on the web?"

"Maybe Princess Kimmie thought hanging up pictures around school was the best way to embarrass Leah in front of all her friends."

Jun nodded, acknowledging Rachel's point. Still, he didn't like it. Kimmie was all about global humiliation.

Posting pictures on a couple dozen lockers didn't have the same impact.

"Please, Rachel," Jun pleaded. "I need to know about Melanie Stevens."

"Melanie who?" Rachel said, draping one arm over the bench's backrest, and looking pleased with herself. The smug look sent Jun's pulse racing. Rachel knew something. He was sure of it. His eyes traced the perimeter of her head. There had to be some way to unlock that vault.

He tried a different approach. "Look, if you don't help me find Melanie, I'm going to get blamed for exposing Kimmie's secret. I'll be just another victim of Kimmie Cole. Are you really going to sit there and let that happen?" The scowl that was Rachel's constant companion thinned, then disappeared. Her face softened too, especially around the eyes.

The vault was opening.

"If you don't help me," Jun pressed, "it'll be another win for Kimmie. Is that what you want? To see Kimmie Cole wreck another kid's life?"

Rachel's eyes darted back and forth as she thought it over. Her mouth opened and she drew a breath that lifted her shoulders slightly. Rachel paused then, considering perhaps how to begin, and Jun, leaning forward, found he was holding his breath. A moment later, Rachel's features tightened again and her scowl returned.

She looked away. "I've got nothing to say."

"But . . ." Jun started.

Rachel had been on the verge of revealing . . . something. But the moment had passed and she'd gone back to being the cover girl for *Stubborn* magazine.

"Come on, Jun," Chris said, prodding him. "There's nothing for us here."

Chris started off and Jun followed reluctantly behind. He looked over his shoulder, hoping to catch Rachel in another vulnerable moment. No such luck. Her mouth was closed and her jaw was set. Chris pulled open the glass door. Jun had one foot in the hallway when Rachel called his name. He turned.

"Saint Mary's," Rachel said. "That's where Mel goes to school." She folded her arms. "But that's all you're getting from me."

Jun nodded briskly. "Thanks, Rachel. You're doing the right thing," he reassured her.

Rachel grimaced. "Just get going, and take your girlfriend with you."

Chris gripped the doorframe. "He is not my BOY-FRIEND!"

Chris's outburst brought Mrs. Kwon into the corridor at the end of the hall. Jun saw her lips move, but couldn't hear her voice over the running photocopy machine.

"We were just leaving," he called out.

Jun pushed Chris out of the office and led her down the hall at a brisk pace to burn off her anger.

"Who does she think she is?" Chris said.

"Keep your voice down," Jun advised as they passed the open door of a sixth-grade classroom. The teacher inside turned from the whiteboard and followed their progress with her eyes. Jun hustled Chris along. In a hushed voice he said, "Give the girl a little credit. She told us where to find Melanie."

"I know, I know," she said, her face flushed red with . . . anger? Embarrassment? It was hard to tell.

"Doesn't it bother you?" Chris asked.

"What?"

"All that boyfriend-girlfriend business?"

Not really, Jun thought. When you're about to be kicked out of school for a crime you didn't commit, getting teased by the likes of Rachel Cook is pretty low on the anxiety list.

"A little," Jun said to make Chris feel better.

"We're just friends. What does it matter that you're a boy?"

Jun shrugged. "Doesn't matter to me."

"Right. You get it, but how do I make Rachel see that?" Chris's hands balled into fists so tight her knuckles cracked.

The sound made Jun squeamish. "Giving Rachel a black eye isn't going to help her *see* any better," he said.

"Yeah, but she deserves one."

After four days of dealing with cyberbullies, Jun found Chris's old-fashioned approach to justice oddly refreshing. "Beating her up won't help," he said. "Rachel will run to the office, and then you'll be the one in trouble."

They detoured through the eighth-grade wing. Halfway to the cafeteria Jun stopped short and pointed to an open classroom door.

"That's Mr. Wainwright's room," he said. "I say we go in and check up on Dion's story about maintaining the website."

"It's probably a lie."

"Chris, we need to go into this with an open mind."

"My mind is open."

"How much?"

Her thumb and pointer finger indicated the amount. About a quarter inch.

"That's what I thought," Jun said. "What do you have against Dion?"

"I just don't trust him. He's so . . ." Chris fumbled for the right word, "untrustworthy."

"Really? I thought he was kind of cool."

"Which part? When he made fun of Mr. Wainwright or when he made fun of me?"

Jun decided not to touch that ticking bomb. "Either way, we need to see if his alibi checks out."

Chris shrugged. "Whatever."

Jun stuck his head inside the classroom. "Excuse me, Mr. Wainwright?"

The teacher sat behind his desk, grading papers. His posture was perfect. Spine straight, shoulders back, eyes angled down through tortoiseshell glasses. The desk was free of clutter, except for a grade book, two stacks of paper, and a plastic cup filled with two dozen felt-tipped red pens. Jun noted that there was no computer. The teaching staff had received brand-new laptops at the beginning of the year. Mr. Wainwright must keep his stowed away somewhere. Jun lost a degree of respect for the man.

There was no response to his initial greeting. Jun crossed tentatively to the desk, Chris following behind. "Mr. Wainwright?" he asked again.

The teacher held up his index finer, signaling them to wait.

The hair on top of Mr. Wainwright's head was white and looked freshly combed. Classical music played softly from an unseen radio.

Mr. Wainwright kept Jun and Chris waiting for another minute as his red pen checked and double-checked the test that lay before him. Mr. Wainwright returned the red pen to the top of the page. He eyed Chris and Jun warily, then lifted a corner of the test, using it as a shield as he wrote the grade.

He needn't have bothered. Once the teacher flipped the

test onto the face-down stack, the grade bled through the backside of the paper. Someone had gotten an A.

Mr. Wainwright took a bag lunch from his desk drawer and pulled out a sandwich, which he placed on a napkin on top of his spotless desk. Finally he looked up and plastered a tight smile on his face. "Now . . . what can I do for you?"

If this were any other day, Jun would apologize for disturbing the teacher's lunch and offer to come back another time. But there was a mystery to solve and time was running like sand through his fingers. "Um . . . we wanted to ask a few questions about Dion Little."

Mr. Wainwright unwrapped his sandwich. "I do not discuss my students with anyone but their parents and the principal."

"This isn't about school. We're here because of Kimmie Cole. Have you heard about the pictures?"

Mr. Wainwright rested his cheek in the palm of his hand. He looked bored by the topic, even though Jun had just introduced it. "It's all my students talk about. But I'm afraid that is a matter best handled by the school's administration."

"Mr. Hastings sent me here. He gave me permission to look into the case."

"Ah . . . you must be *Jun*." Mr. Wainwright's eyes traveled from Jun's face to his sneakers and back again. "I was expecting someone . . . different."

It was the fourth time that week he'd been mistaken for a girl. Jun decided to seriously consider legally changing his name to something more masculine when he was older. Like Rocco, Ox, or Tank.

"Will you answer a few questions?" Jun asked.

"Mr. Hastings informed the staff that we are to offer you whatever assistance necessary to find the cyberbully."

"Okay," Jun said. "Let's start with Dion Little."

"Dion is a student in my seventh block class."

Jun waited for more but Mr. Wainwright did not continue. It was clear that Mr. Wainwright would volunteer nothing. Jun had to drag the information out of him.

"Does he manage your website?" Jun asked.

"Yes."

"How long has he been doing that?"

"Since the second week of September."

Jun glanced around the room to confirm his initial observation. "But you don't even have a computer!"

"At the beginning of the year the school administration insisted the eighth grade teachers get 'on-line,'" Mr. Wainwright said, as if the internet were a passing fad. "Apparently, our students no longer have the cognitive ability to simply write down their homework when they come into class. Thank goodness we have the world wide web to breed further laziness in our already apathetic students."

Jun exchanged a quick glance with Chris. She seemed to be thinking the same thing — the guy was a major technophobe. Jun looked around the classroom. Was the classical music he heard being played on a record player?

"Can you tell me about your website?"

"Dion built the site and maintains it. Its purpose is mainly as a platform to post daily homework assignments, student writing models, and major projects."

"That's a lot of responsibility for an eighth grader," Chris said.

"Mr. Little has provided this service to me, without error, since the beginning of the school year."

"Do you also teach a girl by the name of Kimmie Cole?"

"I do."

"Have you ever seen Dion hanging around her?" Jun asked, hoping to establish a link between the two.

Mr. Wainwright furrowed his brow, then slowly nodded. "Yes. At the beginning of the year, mainly."

"Were they friends?"

Mr. Wainwright tilted his head left then right, weighing his answer.

"Perhaps."

Jun sensed the teacher was holding something back. "More than friends?"

"I don't pay much attention to middle school romances,

Mr. Li. They have the average life span of a carton of milk."

Romance? Now there was an interesting word choice. "Are you saying they were boyfriend and girlfriend?"

Mr. Wainwright shrugged. "I wouldn't know."

Jun searched for a new angle of attack. "How many times did you see them together?"

"Three, maybe four times last month."

"And since then?"

"Mr. Little seems to have fallen off Ms. Cole's radar screen."

A romantic connection between Dion and Kimmie was the last thing Jun expected to hear, and yet if were true, a bad breakup might lead heartbroken Dion to do something drastic — like expose Kimmie's secret.

Jun returned to the same question he'd asked of all the suspects, the only question that really mattered. "Where was Dion during block seven on Friday?"

Mr. Wainwright separated his sandwich into two right triangles. "I've been over this with Principal Hastings," he said curtly.

"Just one more time. Please."

Mr. Wainwright sighed and pointed to a desk in the back corner. "He was there the entire period. No trips to the bathroom or the water fountain. Now if you don't mind," he said looking down at his lunch, "my tuna salad is getting cold." When neither Jun nor Chris laughed,

Mr. Wainwright added dryly, "That was a joke."

Jun's laugh was too loud and arrived too late.

Chris elbowed him and he stopped abruptly.

"Please go," Mr. Wainwright said.

"Just one more question."

"You heard the teacher," Chris said, pushing him from behind.

As he reluctantly started off, Jun caught sight of a falling object. It was Mr. Wainwright's plastic cup, the one filled with red pens. Chris must have knocked it over when nudging him to the door. The cup hit the ground, and the pens exploded in different directions. They skittered across the floor, some making it as far as the door.

"Look at what you did, Jun!" Chris said.

Jun whirled around, eyelids and jaw extended. "Me?"

"Say you're sorry," she demanded.

Even Jun, who often apologized for things that were only partly his fault, thought this was extreme. "But I . . ."

"Say it!"

There was something in the way Chris's eyes bored into him that made him surrender. She was trying to tell him something. He had no idea what, but he decided to play along.

"Sorry, Mr. Wainwright," Jun said, bending to pick up the cup. "I'll take care of this. Right away." Jun scurried from pen to pen, like a squirrel gathering nuts. Grumbling,

Mr. Wainwright got up from his chair and bent over a small pile of pens. Bracing one hand on his knee, he reached down to gather them up.

They worked in silence for several seconds, and Jun, having collected a dozen pens, glanced up looking for Chris. After all, this was her fault. The least she could do was help. Chris had positioned herself in front of the face-down stack of papers on the opposite side of the teacher's desk. At that moment, she was lifting the top paper from the stack to peer at its front side.

Grades were not meant for public viewing. Her actions were in violation of the privacy rules spelled out in the student handbook and punishable by two days of detention. Jun wanted to communicate all of this to Chris. But his desire not to see her caught made him choose a different course of action.

The teacher had his back to Chris. His hand groped for a pen just out of reach. Jun circled in front of him and held out the cup, trying to be helpful. At the same time, he wanted to give Chris an opportunity to slip around the desk without being noticed. Mr. Wainwright straightened and inserted the pen into the cup.

"Found this one under the desk," Chris said, approaching them with a single pen held in the air.

"Thank you, Chris," Jun said, giving her a look that said, *We'll talk about this later.*

"I think it's time both of you left." Mr. Wainwright said. "And Jun, try not to knock over any desks on your way out."

Jun thanked the teacher several times as he backed carefully out the door. Mr. Wainwright waved the gratitude away as if it were a bad smell. When they were halfway down the corridor, Jun said to Chris, "I can't believe you did that! You could have gotten us both detention!"

"I had to be sure."

"Of what?" he demanded.

"I thought I saw the name on the test Mr. Wainwright was grading when we came in."

Jun threw his hands in the air. "What difference does it make who got the A?"

"Two of my brothers had Mr. Wainwright. He's the toughest teacher in the school. For him, As are like Christmas presents. He only hands them out once a year."

Jun was curious about the student, but he knew if he asked, he'd be just as guilty as Chris. He pressed his lips together.

"Don't you want to know who it was?" Chris asked.

Jun folded his arms. Some lines should not be crossed. "No."

"It might have something to do with our investigation."

"Huh?"

"The kid . . . it's someone we've talked to this week."

Jun flipped through his mental slideshow of faces. None seemed to fit. He felt his resistance wavering. He glanced over at Chris. Her face was all business.

"Seriously, you're not gonna believe it."

At this point, he couldn't pass up any bit of new information that might be important to the case. "Okay, tell me."

"Charlie Bruno."

Jun's eyebrows furrowed. "How does he figure into all this?"

"Charlie's got more muscles than brains. I wouldn't expect him to be the one acing Wainwright's test."

"But what's his connection to the pictures? He wouldn't write those mean things about his own girlfriend."

"How should I know? You're the detective."

She was right about one thing. He was the detective. But he didn't have a clue.

They came around the corner and nearly collided with Dion Little. "Watch where you're going, Sherlock," he said. "You almost ran me over."

It would take a great deal more than Jun's ninety-two pounds to knock Dion down. Still, he apologized.

Dion nodded grudgingly. His eyes flicked from Jun's face to Mr. Wainwright's room and back again. "What were you two doing here?"

If Jun stated their true purpose, Dion would know they'd been checking on his story. "We were just on our way to lunch," he said.

"From where?"

"Gym," Jun said and at the same moment Chris blurted, "Chorus."

Dion folded his arms. "Which is it?"

"We were coming from different directions," Chris explained, "but we took the same short cut."

"Uh-huh," Dion said. "So you weren't talking to Mr. Wainwright?"

"Who's Mr. Wainwright?" Jun asked louder than necessary in an effort to show his surprise.

"My English teacher."

"Is his classroom down here?" Jun asked, looking both ways over his shoulders.

"Whatever," Dion said, shaking his head. "I'll see you two around."

Jun waited until Dion was a safe distance away. "Do you think he bought it?"

"Oh yeah. You were real convincing."

"Really?"

"Of course not!" Chris said. "He saw right through you."

Jun grimaced. He'd never been very good at lying, and yet, as a detective, lying seemed to be part of the job. Just one more reason he wasn't qualified.

"What do you think about what Mr. Wainwright said?" Jun asked. "About Kimmie and Dion being a couple?"

"Never work," Chris said decisively.

"Agreed. But one thing's for sure," Jun said. "Dion lied to us about not knowing Kimmie, which means he may have lied about other things."

Jun wished people behaved more like computers. In the most basic programming language, binary, the answer was either one or zero. On or off. Yes or no. People weren't quite so logical. They were full of complexities he didn't understand, which meant their answers to his questions could never be fully trusted.

Tomorrow was Friday. The last full school day for investigation. The problem wasn't a lack of leads. Between Dion Little, Melanie Stevens, Arthur Radley, and now Charlie Bruno, there were simply too many questions and not enough answers.

Monday's deadline loomed closer than ever.

Chapter 11

Jun caught Mr. Hastings in his office at the end of the day.

"I can't talk now," Mr. Hastings said, slipping one arm into his suit jacket. "I'm late for a meeting with the superintendent. Kimmie's mother is giving up on finding the culprit. If we don't provide her with the name of the cyberbully by Monday, she's pressing charges against the school." Mr. Hastings straightened his tie. "So unless you know who's behind all this . . ."

"I just need to ask about one student," Jun said.

Mr. Hastings grabbed his briefcase and strode to the door. "Whoever it is, it'll have to wait."

"Melanie Stevens," Jun blurted out as the principal darted past him.

The principal stopped and turned. His eyes were extra

wide. Jun couldn't tell if it was anger or surprise. Maybe both.

"Mrs. Kwon!"

"Yes, Mr. Hastings," the intercom replied.

"Tell Mr. Steward I'm going to be ten minutes late."

Jun knew he'd struck a nerve if the mere mention of Melanie's name was enough to delay a meeting with the superintendent. He planted himself on the edge of the visitor's chair, bent forward at the waist, hungry for new information.

Mr. Hastings stood in front of the window, rubbing his jaw. Outside, a dozen yellow buses were lined up headlights to tailpipe. The rumbling sounds of their engines slipped through the single open window. Mr. Hastings closed the window, cutting the noise in half. He then turned to Jun with a somber expression.

"Cross Melanie off your list."

"What?"

"She's one of the first people we checked on. Her alibi is rock solid."

"What is it?"

"I can't tell you."

Jun's shoulders slumped. How could he unravel this mystery if Mr. Hastings held back vital pieces of information?

"I don't blame you for being annoyed," Mr. Hastings

said, "but for legal reasons, I can't reveal her whereabouts that Friday. Just know that Melanie has been exonerated."

"Hold on a second." Jun slipped his phone from his pocket and retrieved the field-hockey picture. "On Wednesday I talked to Leah Armstrong and I found this picture on her wall." He handed the phone to the principal. "One minute Leah was all cool and relaxed. Then I asked her about this girl, Melanie Stevens, and she got all defensive. Plus, Melanie's a friend of Kimmie's, someone who knew about her bulimia. If I can talk to her, just for a couple of minutes, she might tell me something new."

The principal closed his eyes and sighed. "Jun, there is absolutely no way Melanie Stevens could have posted those pictures. You'll have to take my word on that."

"But even if she's not the bully, she might know something."

"I can't let you speak to her."

Jun slouched in the chair. He felt like a balloon that had run into the business end of a pin.

The intercom beeped. "Sorry to interrupt, Mr. Hastings." It was Mrs. Kwon. "I've got Dr. Cody on line two."

Mr. Hastings looked up to the ceiling and sighed. "When it rains, it pours," he muttered. To Jun he said, "I have to take this. Close the door on your way out."

Jun paused in the doorway. "Mr. Hastings?"

"Yes?"

He didn't want to ask, but he had to. "Am *I* still a suspect?"

Mr. Hastings pushed a flashing button on the phone. Into the receiver, he said, "Gene, I'll be with you in a moment . . . Alright, thanks." He put the doctor on hold and then fell silent for several seconds, staring at his hands. At last he said, "You remember Principal Edwards?"

"Yes."

"There was some trouble last year with cyberbullying too. Principal Edwards took a lot of heat for the way things were handled."

"What do you mean?"

"I'm not saying it was his fault, Jun. He was a good man, but he was forced into early retirement because of the incident."

This did not bode well, Jun decided. If Mr. Steward, the superintendent, had kicked Principal Edwards out of school over a cyberbullying incident, he wouldn't think twice about booting a lowly seventh grader like Jun.

Mr. Hastings continued, "It's my job to keep this place safe, Jun. Right now, I can't rule anyone out."

Jun had been on this case for four days. He'd conducted interviews, lied to his mother, and for what? The principal still considered him a suspect.

"I didn't do this!" he insisted.

Mr. Hastings's finger hovered over the hold button. "Then find the person who did."

Frustrated, Jun strode out of the office. Mrs. Kwon waved to him on his way out the door. He was too preoccupied to return the wave. Why couldn't Mr. Hastings tell him where Melanie Stevens was last Friday? Why did her location require such secrecy?

Distracted by these questions, Jun took two steps into the hall and ran right into a pair of meaty forearms. They were folded over Charlie Bruno's chest.

Jun stumbled back against the office door, bumping his head right in the same spot he had hit on Monday. A stinging pain radiated from the lump, making his eyelids flutter. Jun rubbed the spot while he looked Charlie over. The big kid's jaw was set. His lips cut a straight line across his face, running parallel to the line formed by his pinched eyebrows.

On Monday, the principal had said he'd take care of Charlie. Jun assumed that meant Charlie would be kept at a safe distance. But today was Thursday. Had his bully-free grace period run out?

"We need to talk," Charlie said.

"Sorry, I'm meeting Chris," Jun said. "You remember her, right? Tall, strong, short temper."

"Now!" Charlie grabbed a fistful of Jun's T-shirt at the shoulder and towed him across the crowded hallway to a corridor adjacent to the gym.

Glancing around, Jun saw that the hallway was empty.

Great, he thought. *No witnesses.*

"Have you figured it out yet, Li?"

"I've um . . . narrowed it down to a few people." Jun said, his voice trembling. "It's . . . uh, just a matter of time."

"You gotta hurry up. Kimmie's sick of staying home. She's back on Monday."

"Oh," Jun said, grimacing. He had hoped to solve this case without talking to Kimmie. Not that talking to her was so frightening. It was more about self-preservation. If he was unable name the cyberbully, he didn't want Kimmie to know the extent of his involvement. Otherwise, *he* might be her next target.

Charlie glanced left, then right, before stepping closer. He didn't put his arm around Jun's shoulder, but the huddle had a private, almost confessional feel to it. The last time they were this close, Jun's head nearly became a permanent fixture in the wall. Jun resisted the urge to turn and run. Charlie wanted to talk. He was Kimmie's boyfriend. He might know something.

"Look, all Kimmie's friends keep coming up to me and they're all like, 'When are you gonna take care of this?' And I'm standing around with my hands in my pockets 'cause I don't know who I'm after."

Jun was unsure how to respond. "Th-that must be hard

for you."

"It's nothing like what Kimmie's going through. She's been bawling her eyes out for a week. She don't deserve to be treated like this."

After the conversations he'd had with Rachel Cook and Leah Armstrong, Jun was pretty sure Kimmie had gotten exactly what she deserved.

"These people," Charlie typed on an invisible keyboard to indicate, Jun guessed, the cyberbullies, "they feel like they can do anything. And the things they're saying, they're not true. Kimmie went to counseling over the summer. She's got her problem under control. All that stuff about puking up her meals . . . it's in the past. I've been trying to tell everybody, but no one listens."

"Um . . . that's gotta be tough on you," Jun tried.

Charlie seemed pleased to have found a sympathetic ear. "That's what nobody seems to get!" His louder-than-expected voice echoed down the empty hallway. "I mean, I'm doing everything I can to make her feel better. I call her every night. I send her funny emails. I even wrote some poetry."

"Poetry?" Jun had trouble picturing big Charlie composing love sonnets.

Charlie's eyes hardened. "You got a problem with that?"

"No, no, girls like poetry."

Like Jun had any idea what girls liked.

"Yeah, they do."

Jun realized then that Charlie, like Rachel Cook, might be able to tell him something the principal couldn't. "Do you know a girl named Melanie Stevens?"

"Course I do," Charlie answered. "She's a bitch."

Jun winced. "That's a little harsh, don't you think?"

"Kimmie's words, not mine."

"Why does Kimmie think she's a . . . b-b-b . . ." Jun couldn't bring himself to say the word. ". . . A bad person?"

"Whatever happened between Kimmie and Mel, it was before I came along."

"When did you start dating?"

"September 18th at 4:30 in the afternoon," Charlie said. "I remember because I'd just gotten out of lacrosse practice and Kimmie was finishing up field hockey at the same time."

Both Kimmie and Charlie played sports that required them to carry big sticks. A match made in bully heaven.

"Kimmie needed a ride home," Charlie said, "but her phone was dead, so I let her use mine. After her call, she said I was her hero and as a reward, she took a picture of herself and saved it on my phone." Charlie smiled to himself. "She should've looked gross, you know? I mean, she'd been running around for two hours. But her face . . ." Charlie looked over Jun's shoulder as if seeing Kimmie again on that September afternoon. ". . . all the sweat made her skin sparkle."

Charlie's lips bunched up then, like he was mulling something over. He studied Jun's face and seemed to make a decision. "Things aren't going so good now between Kimmie and me. She won't return my texts. I'm not sure she wants me around anymore."

A single question had been pushing at the back of Jun's throat for minutes now. "Why do you like her so much?" he asked at last.

Jun worried Charlie would be angry. But the big kid looked confused. It was as if Jun had asked why he liked sports or blue skies or breathing.

"She's the best-looking girl in school," Charlie said as if that explained everything.

"And?" Jun pressed.

Charlie held up his hands. "Look, I know she's posted some mean things online, but she's just joking around. She teases me all the time — that's how I know she cares. Kids at this school, they don't understand her, Jun. Not the way I do. Beneath it all, she's really sensitive."

Just like her boyfriend, Jun thought.

"Anyway," Charlie continued, "I feel like Kimmie's waiting for me to do something. If I can't find out who outed Kimmie, I think . . ." He trailed off.

"What?"

Charlie looked away, sucking in his lips. "I think she

might break up with me."

Jun patted Charlie's arm. It was awkward, soothing his former tormentor, but he knew it was the right thing to do. "It'll be okay."

"Of course it will be okay," Charlie said, suddenly defensive. To emphasize his point, and create a little space, he knocked Jun's shoulder with his fist. The blow made him stumble back. And it hurt.

"Just get me that name before Monday," Charlie demanded.

Jun wondered if any name would do. For Charlie, the issue wasn't finding the bully; it was beating someone up to prove his devotion to Kimmie.

"I'll do my best," Jun said.

Charlie's gaze lifted over Jun's head. "I'm gonna give that kid a pounding he'll never forget."

Jun puzzled over the pronoun choice. "How do you know it's a boy?"

"You know girls, they could never be that mean."

Chris was convinced the culprit was a girl. For Charlie, it was the opposite. Jun remained neutral on the question. From what he'd seen, neither boys nor girls had a monopoly on meanness.

"We'll talk tomorrow," Charlie said. "You're going to have some good news for me by then, right?"

"Sure," Jun said, not feeling sure at all.

"Good." Charlie shuffled off then, knocking his fist lightly against the lockers as he went.

Jun watched him go. Even though Charlie was ready to beat up a random kid to prove his commitment to his girlfriend, Jun felt bad for the eighth grader. He really did care for Kimmie.

Outside, the buses shifted into gear and lumbered out of the circular driveway. Jun stepped to the curb, waving away the gray exhaust. He looked around for Chris. She sat on a nearby bench, biting her fingernails.

Chris's version of a manicure.

"How'd it go with Mr. Hastings?" she asked. "Find anything out?"

"Nothing good."

Jun considered what the principal had told him about Melanie and then weighed it against his strangely emotional conversation with Charlie.

"You got time for another field trip?" Jun asked.

Chris shouldered her backpack and hooked her thumbs under the straps.

"Sure. Where to?"

Jun looked down the road, nervous anticipation bubbling in his stomach.

"Catholic school," he said.

Chapter 12

Saint Mary's was a squat three-story building made of brick and glass. The towering spires of the attached cathedral cast pointed shadows over the school. Jun and Chris stood across the street. They turned their heads left and right to see around the cars and minivans arriving and departing from the curbside.

"Is that her?" Chris pointed to a pair of girls skipping down the long concrete steps. Jun compared the faces of both girls to the picture of Melanie on his phone. Neither seemed to match.

"Which one?"

Chris grabbed Jun's arm to bring the picture closer to her eyes. "Forget it," she said after a second look.

According to Leah Armstrong's picture, Melanie had

blond hair, narrow shoulders, and a long neck. Jun found it nearly impossible to tell one girl from the other. They were all dressed alike — a white blouse, a forest-green vest with an embroidered crest, and a matching pleated skirt that reached past the knees.

"This is like looking for a needle in a box of needles," Jun said.

"Wait here," Chris said, snatching the cell from his hand. Finding a break in the traffic, she hustled across the street and blocked the way of three girls walking down the sidewalk. During their brief exchange, Chris held up the picture. The girl in the middle turned and pointed out a single dark-headed figure striding to the bike rack.

Chris honed in on the solitary girl. Jun dashed across the street to intercept.

"Melanie's a blond," Jun called.

Chris strode purposefully to her target with the phone held in front of her face. Her eyes leapt from the girl to the picture and back again.

Jun didn't understand Chris's confidence until he got closer and saw that the girl's hair wasn't just dark; it was jet black. Jun was no expert on hair dyes, but he was pretty sure that particular shade only came out of a bottle. The girl knelt at the bike rack and spun the dial on her combination lock.

"Are you Melanie Stevens?" Jun asked.

The girl didn't look up. "Unfortunately."

Melanie wore black lipstick, black stockings, and at least two dozen black rubber bracelets on her left wrist. The lipstick, stockings, and bracelets, along with the jet black hair, established a certain tone that was disrupted by Melanie's fingernails. They were painted red and pink, the colors alternating from one finger to the next.

"I'm Jun and this is Chris. We go to Brookfield."

"Sorry to hear that," she said, locating the third number in her combination and popping the lock.

Jun glanced at Chris to see what she made of Melanie's less-than-welcoming response. Even Chris, who wasn't exactly the Queen of Good Manners, seemed surprised by Melanie's attitude.

Finding no traction with his conversation starters, Jun asked simply, "Do you have a minute?"

Melanie stood, brushing pebbles from her knees. "What do you want?" she asked.

"I wanted to talk to you about Kimmie Cole," Jun said. Melanie's face hardened. She pivoted, yanked her front tire from the rack, and straddled the bike. "Never heard of her." She set her right foot on the top pedal, ready to shove off.

Chris grabbed the handlebars. "We just have a few questions."

"Like I care." Melanie walked the bike forward, nudging Chris back.

Chris planted her feet. "Just give us a minute, okay?"

"Let go of my bike!"

"Melanie," Jun spoke softly to defuse the standoff, "you're going to want to hear this."

"Hear what?"

"Last Friday somebody hacked into Brookfield's website and posted pictures of Kimmie Cole."

Melanie stopped pushing. The corners of her dark lips turned ever so slightly into a smile. "Were the pictures nasty?"

"Very."

"Is Kimmie in a lot of pain?"

"She hasn't been to school in almost a week," Jun reported.

"Good," Melanie said with a satisfied nod.

First Rachel Cook, then Leah Armstrong, and now Melanie Stevens. Not a single one of them made an effort to hide their true feelings about Kimmie. It must take a special brand of rottenness to stir up such raw hatred.

"So you were friends with Kimmie?" Jun asked.

"Heavy emphasis on the *were*."

"For how long?"

Melanie looked up at the branches of the overhanging tree. "Since fourth grade, I guess. Kimmie and I sold Girl Scout cookies together. Kimmie was a natural at the job. She wouldn't take no for an answer."

"And you *liked* hanging around with her?" Chris asked.

"At first, yeah." Melanie stared down at her boots. Black hair spilled from behind her ear and shielded her face. "Hanging out with Kimmie . . . I don't know. It was like the sun was always shining on her. People treated her different and when you hung around her, they treated you different too. Like you were special somehow." Melanie sighed. "It's hard to explain."

Jun thought she'd done a good job. Kimmie was a drug and for a time, Melanie had been an addict. Just as Charlie was now. Apparently, Kimmie wasn't happy unless there was someone around to worship her.

"The pictures posted on the school's website exposed the secret behind her eating disorder," Jun said, careful not to be too specific.

"Figures."

"So you knew about it?"

"Let's just say, I knew how Kimmie finished most of her meals." Melanie opened her mouth and stopped short of sticking her finger down her throat. "That's pretty much how I got dumped at this fine learning institution."

"What happened?"

Melanie fidgeted with the black bracelets around her left wrist. "It's stupid."

"We won't tell anyone. Promise."

"It's so not worth talking about."

"Listen," Chris said, "at this point, there's nothing

about Kimmie Cole that would surprise us. We've talked to her former friends. The girl's a virus. She's a wrecking ball," Chris said, cribbing notes from Rachel Cook's rants.

It did the trick. Melanie looked up with a half smile. "Totally."

"So what happened?" Chris asked.

Melanie shrugged. "It seems stupid now, but I was actually worried about her. Kimmie was getting so thin. Like gross-thin, you know? Anyway, when I finally cornered her, she was all sweet and like 'thanks-for-being-such-a-good-friend.' But she told me there was nothing to worry about. She'd puked up her last meal."

"But she hadn't," Jun said.

"A week after our talk, Rachel Cook caught her in the bathroom. There Kimmie was, her head in the toilet . . ."

Chris held up her hands. "We get the picture."

"I was getting worried," Melanie continued. "Puking all the time messes up the inside of your throat, so I told the guidance counselor. And the counselor called Kimmie's mom. And then . . ." Melanie's brown eyes, which had been fixed on Jun's face, lowered. The ends of her lips took a similar downward turn. "Then things got really ugly. Kimmie came after me."

"Did she post a picture of you?" Jun asked.

"I wish I'd gotten off that easy. What she came up with was really ingenious, so there's no way Kimmie thought of it herself."

"What did she do?" Chris asked.

"She texted me," Melanie said as if texting was a crime against humanity.

Jun shrugged. "So?"

"It wasn't just one text, Jun. She got the whole seventh grade to do it. Each kid sent like ten texts."

"Is that why you transferred?"

"If you got two thousand texts telling you what a bitch you were, what would you do?"

Melanie's glaring eyes told Jun that this was a question she did not expect him to answer. Still, her unexpected outburst left him stunned. He tried to imagine what such a tidal wave of negativity would do to a person. Suddenly, the all-black outfit did not seem like such an outrageous choice.

"That must have been hard," Jun said softly.

"It was." Melanie took in her surroundings, then added, "It is."

"But you and Kimmie were friends for three years," Chris said. "How could you stand being around someone so mean all the time?"

"Kimmie wasn't always like this. Something changed with her about a year ago. Right after her parents' divorce."

Jun thought back to the awkward twenty minutes he'd spent in Leah Armstrong's pink bedroom. Leah had mentioned that Kimmie's obsession with the truth had started about a year ago. Same time as the divorce. If Kimmie's parents had been less than honest about their feelings for each other, Kimmie may have decided that from then on, she'd live in a lie-free zone.

Jun refocused his thoughts. Mr. Hastings had called Melanie's alibi rock solid. He wanted to hear it for himself.

"So, where were you on Friday around . . ."

"Look, I may be president of the I-Hate-Kimmie Club," Melanie interrupted, "but that doesn't mean I went after her."

"So . . . where were you last Friday?" he tried again.

Melanie sighed impatiently. "Same place you were — school." She gestured to the kids still streaming down the steps. "And we don't get out until three."

Jun checked his watch for verification. It was 3:11. Mr. Hastings was right. Rock solid.

Melanie walked her bike forward. "Anything else?" she asked, her fuse running short.

"Yeah, what's up with those fingernails?" Chris asked.

Chris's unexpected question caught Melanie off guard. A shy smile crossed her face. She held up one hand for examination. "My mom's idea. She's not a big fan of the dye job."

Familiar with forced makeovers, Chris was sympathetic. "They're not so bad."

"Are you kidding?" Melanie said. "They're horrible."

"It's just the kind of thing my mom would go for." Chris held up a few strands of her hair. "She's taking me to the salon tomorrow."

Melanie winced as if a Band-Aid had been ripped off the hairy part of her forearm. "Eww . . ."

Chris shrugged. "I'll survive."

They made an odd pair. Melanie was thin and pale while Chris radiated strength and good health. And yet, here they were bonding over nail polish.

"Just don't agree to any package deals," Melanie advised, staring down at her multi-colored fingernails. "If you think these are bad, you should see my toes."

Chris's eyes narrowed. "*Nobody's* touching my feet," she grumbled.

Melanie laughed at Chris's reaction, and for a moment Jun caught sight of the dimples he'd seen in the picture. She seemed to catch herself then, and the smile evaporated. She put one foot on the pedal, and she rose out of her seat, ready to push off. But the anti-salon talk must have loosened her up. Before she pedaled away, she said firmly, "It wasn't me, Jun."

He nodded. "I'll let you know if we find anything."

Melanie pedaled out of the protective cover of the tree, weaving in and out of the uniformed girls on the sidewalk. Jun watched her go. "Telling the guidance counselor was the right thing to do," he said to Chris.

"But she paid the price for it," Chris replied. "With all those text messages, it's no wonder she transferred."

Jun nodded, but he wasn't so sure. He could see Melanie taking a few days off, maybe even a few weeks. She'd probably see a counselor, and be encouraged to join some new clubs. But transferring to a new school, a Catholic school no less, was a big move. Had something else happened? Was there something Melanie hadn't told him? Whatever it was, it had transformed the grinning, dimple-cheeked blond in the picture into the stone-faced, black-haired Goth he'd just spoken to.

Jun saw the pattern clearly. Anyone Kimmie Cole touched was permanently altered — and not for the better.

Chapter 13

For once Jun's father escaped the office early and made it home in time for dinner. Jun's mother was usually delighted whenever her husband sailed through the door before 8 p.m. This night she was oddly fidgety. Seated beside her husband at the dinner table, she picked crumbs off the tablecloth and placed them in her napkin. Some were microscopic, others just plain imaginary.

Steam from Mr. Li's noodle soup wafted up and fogged the edges of his glasses. "So I'm doing this code review for a new app," Mr. Li said excitedly, "and the engineer who wrote the code, this guy named Stanton, he comes up to me, and his face is all red. Right away, I can tell he's mad."

Jun sat with his elbows on the table, engrossed by his father's story.

"What was Stanton's problem?" he asked.

"It was my review. I told him that there were several flaws in his code that would affect the scalability and response time of the app. Stanton didn't want to hear it. He said that my comments were too picky and would ruin the elegance of his design. I said to him, just wait until the beta testing, then you'll see."

Jun hung on his every word. "So who was right?"

"I was, of course," Mr. Li said with a laugh. "Stanton just doesn't know it yet."

It sounded like boasting, but when it came to programming, his father did know everything. That was why he could never get out of work at a reasonable hour. He loved his job, and he was exceptionally good at it. A victim of his own success.

His mother cleared her throat. Caught off guard by the sound, Mr. Li straightened in his chair. He erased his smile and attempted to duplicate her grave demeanor.

His mother gripped his father's hand. Jun knew then something was up. It was a move she almost never made unless she was about to have a "difficult" conversation.

Maybe his father being home wasn't a coincidence after all.

"Jun, you've been getting in later than usual this week," his mother said. "Anything you want to tell us?"

Jun recognized the forced civility in her voice. She

knew something and she was giving him a chance to fess up! But what? What did she know? It had to be about Kimmie. What else could be important enough to summon his father home from work?

"Um . . ." he began, stalling for time. "I'm not really sure what you're talking about."

"We know your secret, Jun," Mrs. Li said almost evenly. "You might as well tell us."

Mr. Hastings must have called! Jun felt betrayed. The principal had given him until Monday, and just because Jun was still clueless on Thursday night, that didn't mean Mr. Hastings had the right to rat him out.

"Jun . . ." his mother pressed, her patience wearing thin.

Trapped, he took a deep breath. "I don't know where to begin."

"Just tell us. Are you dating Melanie Stevens?"

"WHAT?"

"You heard me."

Jun blinked and shook his head. "I barely know Melanie."

"You could've fooled me," Mrs. Li snapped. "The last ten websites you visited were all about Melanie Stevens."

Jun's anxiety turned to indignation. "You checked my web browser?"

Mrs. Li looked away and her tone softened. "I didn't

mean to. But after our conversation yesterday, I was curious. So I used your computer and conducted a search. And what did I find? All the links for Melanie Stevens had already been clicked."

His mother's presumption that they were dating was completely preposterous, and yet it offered a way out. As much as Jun hated piling one lie on top of another, he had to seize the opportunity.

"Uh, yeah. We're sort of seeing each other."

A loud slap on the table made the silverware jump. "Way to go, Jun! She's a knockout," his father said, beaming with pride.

"Jon, please," his mother hissed.

Jun understood his father's reaction. One internet picture featured Melanie sprinting toward the goal in her field hockey uniform. Her blond hair trailed out behind her, but it was her long, athletic legs that drew the eye. Jun was thankful that Melanie's current look (black on black on black) was nowhere to be found online.

His mother's eyes bored into him. "On Monday, I told you how worried I was about the internet and today I find out you're using it to meet girls!"

"I didn't meet Melanie online."

His mother's narrowed eyes looked skeptical. "Then how did you meet?"

"Chris introduced us," Jun said, remembering that

Chris had reached Melanie before him. Half-truths were pretty much all he had left.

"Does Melanie play for the Hornets?'"

"No, she doesn't go to Brookfield. She transferred last year. She's at Saint Mary's now."

Mrs. Li's eyebrows rose. "Saint Mary's?" She leaned back, absorbing this new information. "Really?"

Saint Mary's was a respectable private school. Not on par with Wellington, but in the same league.

"What did you talk about?" Mrs. Li pressed.

"Huh?"

"When you met. What did you talk about?"

Jun recalled the conversation. Cyberbullies, bulimia, and text-message attacks . . . all that romantic stuff.

"School," he said simply.

His mother seemed to approve of this answer. "So it's not serious?"

"We're just getting to know one another, Mom. That's why I visited those websites. I was checking up on her."

"We do the same at work," his father pointed out, "when someone applies for a job."

Jun smiled at his father, thanking him for the assist.

"And you didn't meet her online?" Mrs. Li asked again, though the edge was gone from her voice.

"No, Mom," Jun said. "We met in the real world. Face to face."

Mrs. Li settled back into her chair, her shoulders relaxing. She adjusted her placemat so its sides were at right angles with the table's edge. Eyes downcast, she said, "Thanks for your honesty, Jun."

Jun sank slightly lower in his chair. *Anytime*, he thought miserably.

Mrs. Li lifted her water glass, and seeing that it was empty, rose from the table. "Does anyone need a refill?"

Jun shook his head. His father did the same. Mrs. Li excused herself and left the table for the kitchen. She stopped in the doorway and turned.

"By the way, any word on those recommendation letters?"

The word from both teachers had been *No*.

"I'm still waiting to hear."

"Stay on it. I don't want your new girlfriend distracting you from the application process."

"Okay," Jun said, his face feeling as hot as his soup.

Once Mrs. Li was gone, Jun's dad turned to him. The smile he'd been suppressing blossomed on his face. "A field hockey player, huh?" He reached across the table and delivered an atta-boy to Jun's shoulder.

Jun thought of the dyed hair and the black bracelets on his would-be girlfriend. "Yeah," he said, "lucky me."

Chapter 14

Friday

The next morning, Jun sat beside his father at the kitchen table. Mr. Li held a coffee mug just inches from his mouth, ready to take a sip whenever he looked away from the paper.

Jun's eyelids were heavy from lack of sleep. He stared longingly at his father's mug. "Can I have some too?" he asked.

His father looked up, surprised. "What, coffee?"

"Yes, please."

"Sure!" Mr. Li said, leaping to his feet.

Jun guessed this must be part of a natural progression in his father's eyes. First, Jun dates girls. Next, he wants coffee. By the end of the week, he'll be asking for a razor and a can of shaving cream.

Mr. Li poured the coffee at the counter then set the cup on the table with a dramatic flourish. "Sugar?" he asked.

"I'll take it black."

This seemed to impress his father all the more. Little did his dad know that it wasn't the coffee Jun wanted but the caffeine. For the second night in a row, Jun had crept downstairs after midnight to use the computer.

Dion was the subject of his first search. Like Melanie Stevens, Dion had created his own website. There were lots of pictures. Dion went for the gangster look. Half-lidded eyes, chin raised, lips sucked in, like he was raised on the streets of South Central L.A., instead of a cushy middle-class suburb in Massachusetts.

Scrolling down, Jun found a single picture that featured a smile. A grinning Dion held the Laser XL2 next to his cheek. Jun burned with jealously over the newly released smartphone. But something wasn't right. Dion's after-school job was managing Mr. Wainwright's website. Weekly salary — zero dollars. So where'd he get the cash?

The other clue Jun had uncovered during his interview with Dion was the name Arthur Radley. An internet search revealed a variety of Arthur Radleys. One was a Baptist minister from New Jersey. Another was a travel agent living in Minnesota. There were Arthur Radleys that sold car insurance, refinished old furniture, and sang songs at kids' parties. There was even a character named Arthur Radley in an old black-and-white movie called *To Kill a Mockingbird*. None of the Arthur Radleys, however, lived anywhere near Brookfield, and therefore they had no relevance to the case that Jun could see.

The next person of interest was Melanie Stevens. He bypassed her personal websites and focused on the text-message attack. The incident was written up in the *Brookfield Times*. The attack occurred on June 13th. Six days before school ended. That day, Melanie had received 2,274 text messages. At the time of the article's writing, June 15th, no disciplinary action had been taken by the school. The problem? Hundreds of kids were complicit in the attack.

Jun remembered the incident now. His mother had mentioned it over dinner one night. But the story hadn't stuck. It was yet another parental warning about the dangers lurking outside his home. If Jun heeded all his mother's warnings, he would never go online; never leave the house without sunscreen; never eat in a fast food restaurant; and never wear shorts in the summer for fear of ticks. Her warning about the text message attack had gone in one ear and out the other.

The last article of the night — day actually, because by then it was 1:30 in the morning — focused on the retirement of Principal Edwards. *The Brookfield Times* speculated that the text message attack was the reason for the longtime principal's retirement. According to the article, the principal's last day was August 18th. Nearly two months after the attack.

Jun frowned. Pieces of the puzzle were still missing.

The caffeine, plus the walk to school, got his blood pumping. By the time he walked through the school's double doors, he was fully awake. A few students milled around the hallways, unpacking their backpacks or waiting for a homeroom teacher to unlock the door.

Jun had just hung his jacket inside his locker when someone grabbed his shoulder and whirled him around. He expected Charlie Bruno. Manhandling Jun was what the eighth grader did best. But it wasn't Charlie who glared down at him.

"Not so tough now," Rachel Cook snapped.

She shuffled closer. Jun pressed against the lockers to keep her stomach from touching his chest.

"Nobody calls me a fat pig and gets away with it."

"I-I never called you . . ."

"The principal might think different once I show him this." Rachel held up a folded piece of paper.

It was your standard 8½" by 11" computer paper. Yet Rachel treated it like a smoking gun, proof of some terrible crime he'd committed.

Jun reached for the paper. "Let me see that."

Rachel held the sheet behind her back. "So you can

destroy the evidence? I don't think so."

"You've got the wrong guy!" Jun cried.

"Yeah? How many boys named Jun do we have at this school?"

She had a point. More curious than ever, Jun reached around Rachel to grab the paper. He wished for Chris's long arms . . . actually, he wished for Chris herself. She'd wrestle that paper from Rachel without breaking a sweat.

Jun grabbed hold of Rachel's wrist and tried to shake the paper loose. With her free hand, Rachel shoved him, hard. Jun slammed into the lockers, whacking that small, tender lump on the back of his head. Three times in one week — what a marksman! Jun released Rachel's arm to rub away the fresh wave of pain.

Rachel strode off. She'd taken only a half-dozen steps when she stopped and turned. "You know what's funny? I always thought you were kinda cool. Different from the others." Her eyes narrowed. "But you're just like the rest. And once they see this" — she held up the paper and shook it — "they'll kick you out of school for sure." She lumbered off in the direction of the main office.

"But I didn't do anything!" he yelled.

Jun chased after her. He needed to see what was written on that paper. Perhaps examining it — the word choices, the sentence structure, the punctuation — might give him a clue as to the actual author.

He'd almost gotten within shoulder-tapping range when a kid moving in the opposite direction slammed into him. The blow spun Jun around.

The kid was tall and lanky with a thick silver chain around his neck. "Watch where you're going, *Junie*."

It wasn't the shoulder bump that bothered Jun, though that had hurt. It was that the silver-chained kid knew his name. And the way he said it, like they were bitter enemies. Jun had seen the kid around. Another eighth grader. But Jun certainly didn't know *his* name.

Jun muttered a half-hearted apology to Silver Chain and turned to scan the hall for Rachel. She was nearly at the end of the corridor. "Wait!" he called. His voice triggered the opposite reaction. Her stride lengthened and she disappeared around the corner.

Students began to pour through the doors, filling the corridor. A bus had arrived, maybe two. Jun darted around the kids, his sneakers squeaking. Rounding that same corner, he stumbled to a stop. Rachel was nowhere to be seen. The office was at the very end of this hallway. Rachel would've had to break Olympic records to reach her destination without being spotted.

Jun had only a moment to ponder this mystery before the sounds of muffled shouting drew his attention to a nearby exit. Through the door's rectangular glass window he could see outside. Two kids were fighting. One of them was a girl, extra tall with long brown hair.

Chris!

Jun darted left and threw the door open. The shouting doubled in volume. Chris had a boy in a headlock. But that wasn't all. She was using the boy as a shield to keep two other boys from rushing her.

"Just try it," Chris yelled to her attackers.

One kid, the bigger of the two, advanced. Chris took the boy in the headlock, rolled his head into her stomach, then shoved him off with two hands like he was a basketball and she was making a forward pass. The kid hit the others and all three went down.

Chris presided over the tangle of arms and legs. "You got anything more to say?"

The boys scrambled to their feet and dashed off. The one in the middle, the human basketball, ran drunkenly across the lawn. His friends on either side kept correcting his crooked course.

Jun pushed his way through a circle of onlookers to help.

Chris must've mistaken his advance for another attack. Pivoting, she grabbed two fistfuls of Jun's jacket, bringing him to the tips of his toes.

"It's me! It's me!"

The wrinkles in Chris's forehead smoothed and her arms relaxed, setting Jun back down. "Don't come at me like that!"

The door swung open. A sixth-grade teacher, Mr. Castle, filled the doorway. "What is going on here?" he boomed.

The crowd quickly dispersed. Jun led Chris away by the elbow, keeping to the concrete path to find a new entryway into the building.

"What happened?" he asked.

"I don't know," Chris said, retying her ponytail. "One minute I'm walking to school, minding my own business and the next, these sixth graders are all in my face asking if you're my friend. So I'm like yeah, I'm Jun's friend, and then they want to know if you're my boyfriend . . ." Chris daintily tucked a stray lock behind her ear. "Then things got a *little* out of control."

Jun held the door open for Chris as they reentered the school. "Did they say anything else?"

"Something about a nasty email you sent to the whole school."

First, Rachel Cook. Then Silver Chain. Now this. A pattern had emerged, and if the first ten minutes of school were any indication, things were about to get a whole lot worse.

"I need to check my school account!" Jun cried, jogging ahead. "I'm going to the library."

"It doesn't open until first block."

Jun whirled around. "I need to get online right now."

"Hang on." Chris marched down the hall and stiff-armed the door to the girls' bathroom. She came out a few moments later holding a smartphone. A short sixth grader followed her out. Her jaw hung open so wide Jun could see her pink braces. "Give it back!" she shrieked.

"Relax," Chris said. "I'm just borrowing it."

Jun's desire to return the phone to the distressed sixth grader was outweighed by his anxiety over his predicament. If he was right, and he had a strong suspicion he was, this was big, big trouble. Good manners had to take a backseat.

"It will only take a minute," he said, trying to reassure her.

Braces folded her arms and huffed loudly.

Taking the phone, Jun worked his way through the various menus until he came to his school email account. The account had been issued back in sixth grade. It was used to communicate with teachers and to hand in assignments digitally. Jun quickly entered his screen name and password.

He expected fifty, maybe a hundred emails. But the sight of two hundred and sixty-three new messages made his breath catch in his throat. And judging by the subject headings, they weren't fan letters.

Chris read the first one on the list. "You're a tiny, worthless . . ." she broke off at the profanity. "Whoa! That's a bit much."

"Open that one," Braces said, reading over Jun's other shoulder.

"Mind your own business," Chris snapped.

"It's *my* phone."

Jun couldn't argue that point. He opened the email the sixth grader had indicated. It had the comparatively tame subject heading: DISAPPOINTED.

I've known u since the 2 grade. I always thought u were a bit of a geek, but a nice geek. So how could you say those things about Kimmie and Rachel? I guess I never really knew what kind of a jerk u were.

A mass mailing like this one prompted Melanie Stevens to transfer schools. Was that the next step for Jun? He tried to picture himself in a Catholic school uniform. Scratchy blazer, dress pants, striped tie. No thank you. Thankfully, Jun had only received about ten percent of the messages Melanie had.

"Wow, people really hate you," Braces said, almost admiringly.

"I've been set up!" Jun insisted. "Someone must've posed as me online."

"Hey!" Chris stabbed a finger at the screen. "What's that one?"

The subject heading read:

Shut up about your girlfriend.

Jun recognized that email for what it was — a nuclear bomb. "We can't go through all these right now."

"OPEN IT!" Chris demanded.

"Yeah, open it," Braces added.

Reluctantly, Jun tapped open the message.

Please keep the private parts of your life private. Nobody wants to hear about how in love u r with Chris Pine.

A wide smile split the sixth grader's face. "Are you guys dating?"

"No," both replied simultaneously. Chris's voice, however, was much louder than Jun's. The red flush creeping up her neck reminded Jun of the rising mercury in a thermometer.

It occurred to him that the messages clogging his account were all replies. The original message, the one he supposedly sent, must also be attached. He scrolled down and read the single letter that triggered the email avalanche.

Listen up,

By now we've all seen the pictures that outed Kimmie Cole, and there's been a lot of talk about how those pictures appeared online. Well, the debate ends today. I, Jun Li, confess — I posted the pictures on the school's website.

Let's face it, Kimmie got exactly what she deserved. She's the bitchiest cyberbully this school has ever seen! Just think about Rachel Cook. Everyone knows she's a big, fat pig. We don't need the likes of Kimmie Cole to point that out to us. Kimmie's observations are obvious and her intentions are cruel, so I gave her a taste of her own medicine.

I did what had to be done. Even if I am expelled, and all my friends turn their backs on me, I know my girlfriend, Chris Pine, will always stand by me. We're crazy about each other and her love is all I need. (Of course, it doesn't hurt that she's a great kisser.)

Many of you are too stupid to fully comprehend what I've accomplished here, so I'll spell it out in simple terms — I have made the school safer for everyone. You may not understand it today, but someday you'll thank me.

Sincerely,
Jun Li

Jun pinched his eyes shut and turned his head away from the phone. It was bizarre, not to mention a little disorienting, to see his name attached to words that were not his own. The identity thief was like a ventriloquist. And Jun was the dummy!

Even Braces, whom Jun was starting to like, snatched the phone from Jun's hand and said, "You are a jerk!" She scurried away, looking back over her shoulder to see if Chris would follow.

Chris started after her. Jun grabbed her arm. "Forget

her. We've got bigger problems."

Chris scanned the hallway. "We should get out of here. Another attack could come from anywhere."

"Right."

Even as Jun said this, he could feel his spirits lifting. The puzzle pieces were falling into place. A smile spread across his face.

Chris shot him a confused look, like he was grinning at a funeral.

"What are you so happy about?" she demanded.

Jun was nodding now. "If someone went to all this trouble, we must be getting close to the truth."

Chapter 15

On the way to homeroom someone knocked Jun's books from his hands. The rings of his binder popped open upon impact and papers flew everywhere, turning the green tiles a snowy white. He dropped to his knees to gather his things, triggering the unofficial start of the We-Hate-Jun parade. Kids marched by him, saying things like:

"What a stuck-up jerk you are!"

"Kimmie was bad, but you're worse."

"It's been nice knowing you."

That last one was said sarcastically, but Jun was unsure if the kid hinted at his impending expulsion or the fact that kids were ready to tear him limb from limb.

Did it make any sense that Jun, an honor-roll student, a recipient of the perfect-attendance award, would write such a terrible email? Apparently the other students thought it did, because many of those in the We-Hate-Jun parade accompanied their words with kicks that sent his unrecovered books skipping further down the hall.

Between blocks three and four, while picking up his books for the second time that day, a girl he'd never seen before stopped to ask if Chris was a good kisser. This kicked off a wave of giggles from the two girls behind her.

From Jun's perspective, kneeling on the floor, all three girls looked extra tall. Amazons in skinny jeans. He pretended not to hear the question. His red face must've emboldened the lead girl because once he'd collected his books, she followed him all the way to class, buzzing in his ear like a persistent mosquito, asking him if he'd gotten to second base with Chris.

Their "relationship" was Chris's least favorite topic. If she'd been peppered with questions like the ones he'd endured all morning, she had to be ready to explode. Jun felt sorry for her and for anyone who was in the blast zone when she finally went off.

In math, Jun finished his worksheet with three minutes to spare. He spent the rest of the time watching the clock. Were there really only twenty-four hours in a day? With the creeping pace of the second hand, Jun guessed it would take triple that time for a whole day to pass.

He needed to get home and type out an apology letter.

He felt confident that a mass apology letter explaining the identity theft, combined with the weekend off from school, would be enough for most kids to forgive or forget.

One minute now. The end of class brought him that much closer to getting home, but at the same time, Jun feared the bell. It took him away from the security of the classroom and plunged him into the hallway, which was about as safe as crossing a minefield on a pogo stick.

Relax, he told himself. Passing time in the hallway lasted only three minutes. He could survive three minutes. Plus, Chris's science class was just down the hall. Once he picked her up, ninety percent of the bullies would steer clear of him. And the ten percent that didn't would wish they had.

Five . . . four . . . three . . . two . . . one.

Beeeeep!

Jun tried to exit the class two times and on both attempts kids shoved him out of the way. The first time, Jun stepped aside and waved to the door in an *after-you* gesture. The second shove was harder, and his good manners evaporated.

"Don't believe everything you read online," he snapped.

The shover kept walking as if Jun had said nothing.

Bullies, he noted, had selective hearing.

The classroom cleared. Jun stepped out and looked to the right for Chris. Her head usually bobbed above the others in the hall. A growing commotion, however, pulled his attention in the opposite direction. A kid was plowing down the center of the hall, knocking others out of the way.

A girl shrieked. Books tumbled. Curses were muttered.

At last, the crowd parted and Jun could see the bull-dozer.

He should have known.

The teasing, the shoving, the insults — all of it had distracted him from the real threat.

Charlie Bruno emerged from the crowd. His darting eyes were wide and crazed, and when they fell on Jun, they hardened. Target acquired.

Jun turned to run, but Charlie lunged and seized him by the nape of his neck. The crushing pressure of Charlie's hand stopped Jun's feet. Jun reached back to pry away Charlie's fingers. No luck. The eighth grader's grip was pit-bull tight. Charlie spun him around and steered him through the halls, away from his math class, away from Chris. All the other students got out of the way. Some even flattened themselves against the lockers to let Charlie and Jun pass.

Charlie steered him to an empty classroom and pushed him inside. He closed the door quietly behind him, so as not to attract any attention. All doors in the school had a narrow rectangular window. It was his one chance for rescue. That is, if Chris could figure out which of the twenty-five classrooms on the first floor he'd been shoved into.

Jun backed away, holding up his hands. "Whatever you read, it wasn't true."

Charlie advanced. "Shut up!"

"I mean it. Somebody pretended to be me online."

"I'm not listening to you anymore."

"But I didn't write that email last night!"

Charlie stopped. Jun hoped he'd given the bully something to consider. But Charlie paused only to withdraw a piece of paper from his pocket. He unfolded it with shaking hands and read aloud, "Let's face it, that bitch Kimmie got exactly what she deserved." Charlie scanned down the page. "I gave her a taste of her own medicine."

Jun's backside bumped up against the radiator. His retreat was at an end. "I didn't write any of that!" he yelled. "Charlie, take a deep breath and think about this."

"I'm done thinking."

"Wh-why would I agree to help you, then go online and brag about outing Kimmie? Don't you see what this means?" Jun's voice pitched higher. "I'm being set up! The real cyberbully is still out there. If you beat me up, you'll never know who really went after Kimmie."

Plus it will really hurt, Jun thought.

Charlie stopped and held up his evidence. "But you confessed. I've got it right here."

"Those aren't my words."

"It's got your name at the bottom."

"That's my name but my name isn't me," Jun said, unsure if he was making any sense.

Charlie crumpled the paper into a ball and threw it at Jun. The projectile hit him in the face with surprising force. If a single sheet of paper hurt that much . . .

Oh crap!

Charlie seized Jun's T-shirt, pivoted, and then threw Jun into the rows of desks. Jun's left hip landed on top of the nearest desk and he cartwheeled over, hitting the floor shoulders first. He ended up on his back with his legs over his head. Not exactly a strong defensive position. If Charlie wanted to kick his butt, well . . . there was no better time.

The eighth grader marched down the aisle, fists balled.

Jun righted his legs and crab-walked backwards. A forest of steel desk legs blocked his escape. Charlie hauled him to his feet. His mouth opened, and he looked like he wanted to say something. His boiling anger must have gotten the better of him. He threw a punch instead.

The blow connected with Jun's stomach, doubling him over. Charlie grabbed a fistful of T-shirt and straightened Jun up.

Jun studied his attacker through blinking eyes. If the angle of Charlie's cocked fist was any indication, the next punch was going right to his face.

And probably straight on through.

Jun wanted to reason with Charlie. But that first punch had knocked the talk right out of him. He did the only thing he could — he squeezed his eyes shut.

Jun felt Charlie's body jerk forward.

Here it comes!

Jun winced, but there was no impact. Peeling open one eye, he saw Chris behind Charlie, holding back his fist. Chris grabbed a handful of Charlie's hair with her free hand, leaned back, and spun him away.

Charlie pedaled backward and knocked into the teacher's desk. A framed picture on the desk collapsed with a loud smack.

"This isn't your business," he grunted, rubbing the back of his head.

"You've got the wrong guy," Chris said.

Someone else appeared in the doorway. Jun hoped for a teacher, or any responsible adult who might end this situation. No luck. It was another big kid. A friend of Charlie's, most likely.

"Teacher's coming," he said.

Charlie stabbed his finger at Jun. "After school, you're dead." The finger shifted to Chris. "And if you don't stay out of the way, you're dead too."

Chris pressed her hands to her face. "Ooh, I'm so scared."

Charlie remained only long enough to shoot Chris an angry glare before rushing into the hall. Jun wanted to do the same, but something inside his chest didn't feel right. He leaned against a desk, pressing one hand against his ribs, hoping some vital organ hadn't ruptured.

Chris slid behind Jun, put her hands on his shoulders, and steered him to the classroom door. "We gotta get gone."

Still gripping his side, Jun plodded along, each step sending a shock wave of pain rippling through his body.

Send up the white flag, he thought. *I surrender.*

Chapter 16

The last bell of the day rang. Jun remained seated, even after the other students had left. He felt like an inmate on death row waiting to be escorted to the electric chair. Only instead of the warden coming for him, it would be Charlie Bruno. He wondered which was more painful: being electrocuted or getting beaten to a pulp.

"Jun?"

It was his science teacher, Mrs. Cay. She stood beside the door, her bag hanging off her shoulder, her coat over her arm. When there was no response, she said, louder, "Jun?"

He snapped back to reality. "What? Sorry."

"I've been calling your name."

"Sorry," he said again.

"I'm off to daycare." The teacher studied his face, then

pursed her lips. "You alright?"

His ribs ached, the whole school hated him, and Charlie Bruno had promised to end his good-for-nothing life. "I'm fine," he said.

Mrs. Cay looked like she wanted to question him further, but after a glance at the wall clock, she left instead, waving her goodbye over her shoulder.

Jun gathered his books. Confessing to Mrs. Cay wouldn't have helped. The only protection she could offer was from the main office, but thanks to Rachel Cook's printed "evidence" that was the one place Jun dared not go.

In each successive block, he had expected the inevitable intercom page that would summon him to account for his supposed crimes. Yet the page had never come. What was Mr. Hastings waiting for? Rachel Cook's early-morning visit should have triggered swift action from the administration. Her folded sheet of paper proved, beyond any doubt, that Jun was the cyberbully. What more did the principal need?

Jun rose from his desk and walked slowly to the door, each step bringing him closer to his first real fight. Could it even be called a fight? Charlie was so strong and fast, there'd be just two hits. Charlie would hit Jun, and Jun would hit the floor.

He stopped at the door and sucked in a breath to summon his courage. Suddenly, a pair of hands reached out and hauled him into the hallway.

"Arrggghhh!" Jun yelled.

"Shhh!" Chris hissed.

When Jun's heart came unstuck from his throat, he caught his breath and said, "A little warning would've been nice."

"No time," she said, her eyes scanning the hall. "I gotta smuggle you out of here."

The buses had departed some minutes before. Chris and Jun wove around the remaining students, trying not to call any attention to themselves, but with Jun being so short and Chris being so tall, they were a hard pair to overlook. Heads turned as they passed.

They neared the end of the corridor, and Chris's pace quickened. Over her shoulder she said, "We avoid the main exits. We'll slip out through the gym and no one will notice. From there we can run across the soccer field, cut through the woods, and come out somewhere on Washington Street."

Chris rounded the corner before Jun could offer his reluctant agreement. He jogged to catch up, wincing, one hand pressed against his sore ribs.

Nearing the gym, Jun realized the beauty of Chris's plan. Normally at this distance he'd hear the squeaking of sneakers and the *thump-thump-thump* of basketballs emanating from the gym, but with Coach Brown sick and practices canceled, the gym offered a quick and easy escape.

Three-quarters of the way down the hall, Jun became aware that someone was following them. Checking over his shoulder, he spied the distant shape of Rachael Cook. Her pace was relaxed. Decidedly unhurried. No way she would catch them strolling along like that! And yet, there was something about her low-speed pursuit that Jun found unnerving.

Rachel withdrew her phone and pressed it to her ear.

Jun made Chris aware of their tail. They hurried to the wide double doors that marked the entrance to the gym. Chris yanked the door open and the two raced across the wooden floor; the sound of their steps echoed off of the cavernous ceiling.

Jun fixed his eyes on the bright exit sign a hundred feet ahead. The metal door beneath the sign was slightly ajar; a narrow beam of yellowish light streamed through, cutting a long diagonal line across the gymnasium floor. Chris sped forward, ready to shove the door open.

The door opened before she could reach it.

Charlie Bruno stood in front of them, smiling triumphantly. Jun realized then how foolish he'd been. Rachel had herded them, like sheep, right to the slaughterhouse.

Rachel circled slowly around and stood beside Charlie. All day Jun had wondered why he hadn't been called down to the office. Now, seeing the two together, he understood.

"I guess you never met with Mr. Hastings," he said to Rachel.

"I thought about it," she said. "Then I bumped into Charlie. I decided to let him handle things."

The worst the office could do was expel Jun. For those he had supposedly wronged, which seemed to be everybody, having Charlie beat the snot out of Jun was the more attractive option.

Jun remembered his earlier encounter with Charlie and the muscles around his ribs ached anew. He needed a plan, a way to escape, and he needed it two seconds ago!

Jun grabbed Chris's arm. "Stall him," he whispered, pulling out his cell.

"No problem," she said, smirking.

Chris was actually looking forward to this showdown. In her mind this was how problems ought to be solved. Man to (wo)man.

Charlie advanced. Chris met him halfway and planted herself in his path. Charlie faked a move to his right then darted left. Chris was not fooled. Years of basketball had sharpened her reflexes. She dodged to the right, stopping him. Charlie then dashed to his right and Chris shuffled to the left. Despite his threats earlier in the day, Charlie seemed reluctant to lay a hand on her.

Chris had no such gender restrictions.

She delivered a mighty two-handed shove. "Back off, Bruno."

Charlie stumbled back. His wide-eyed surprise quickly transformed into anger. "I don't want to hurt you!"

"I don't want to hurt you either," Chris shot back.

Jun glanced up from his phone where he'd been sending a text and spied Rachel creeping closer to Chris. Before Jun could shout a warning, Rachel rushed forward, her forearms crisscrossed, and smashed into Chris's shoulder. Chris was the stronger of the two, but Rachel had momentum on her side. The collision knocked Chris off balance, clearing an open lane for Charlie to get to Jun.

Jun backpedaled, but he wasn't quick enough. Charlie lunged and grabbed Jun's shirt with a rock-solid fist.

"You don't want to do this," Jun said.

"Standing up to a bully is the only way to make him stop."

It took Jun a second to realize that he was the bully in this scenario.

Could things be any more mixed up?

Charlie drew Jun in, then shoved him hard. Jun stumbled back two steps before landing on his butt. Crab-walking would do no good now. The gym was much too large and there was no place to hide.

Charlie was about to launch a kick that would connect with Jun's bruised ribs when a muffled chime stopped him.

Jun knew the sound emanated from Charlie's phone.

"You should get that," Jun said with a growing confidence.

"It can wait," Charlie growled.

"It's your girlfriend," Jun said.

Charlie was torn. He longed to finish what he'd started, but even the suggestion that Kimmie had texted him was enough to give Charlie pause.

Jun knew it was Kimmie because one minute before he'd sent this text:

Have info about cyberbully will share if u call off charlie need answer asap.

Not exactly great literature, but it was the best Jun could do under the circumstances.

Kimmie might be a cold-blooded snake, but she wasn't stupid. She'd know that Jun wasn't behind this. For one thing, Jun had no personal connection to Kimmie and therefore no motive. And besides, the person who exposed her secret had to know about Kimmie's bulimia, a fact Jun hadn't discovered until after the pictures were posted. Kimmie had absolutely no reason to encourage this fight.

Whether she cared enough to do anything about it — that was another matter.

Curiosity overpowered Charlie's thirst for revenge. Without taking his eyes off Jun, he reached into his back pocket and withdrew his phone. Pivoting away from Jun,

Charlie cupped his hand over the phone and read the message. Jun saw his face in profile. The look of malice dissolved, replaced by a grudging resignation. Charlie shoved his phone back into his pocket, and raising his hands, he backed away.

Rachel and Chris ceased their wrestling.

"That's it?" Rachel said. "You're gonna let him go?"

"Kimmie says he's not the guy."

"But what about the letter?" she huffed.

"Are you deaf? Kimmie says he's not the guy."

"If it were me," Rachel said, "I'd make sure Jun got what was coming to him. You know, just in case."

"You want back on Kimmie's bad side?" Charlie asked. "I'm not stopping you."

Rachel's lack of response signaled a clear no. Kimmie wielded an impressive amount of power in this school, Jun realized, even when she wasn't in the school.

"This isn't over, Li," Charlie said as he backed out of the gym.

Unable to think of a snappy comeback, Jun said, "Okay."

Chris offered up a high five. Jun slapped her hand.

"Smart thinking," she said.

Glowing from the compliment, Jun gazed down at his phone. Forget the pen and the sword, the phone was the mightiest weapon!

Jun was about to offer up this joke when his phone suddenly vibrated. He flinched, startled, and it slipped from his hand.

Chris scooped it up and handed it back. "Do you think it's Kimmie?" she asked.

Jun was sure it was. He read the text.

My house 3:30 dont be late.

Chapter 17

Jun and Chris pushed through the double doors into a bright, cool autumn day. With the threat neutralized, they abandoned their plans to race across the soccer field. Instead, they walked around the front of the school. As they neared the traffic circle, Chris stopped short.

"Oh no," she said.

Jun followed her gaze. The Pine family minivan sat beside the curb, engine running. Almost immediately, the driver's side door flew open and Mrs. Pine strode around the front end of the car.

"Where have you been?" she barked at Chris. "I've been sitting out here for twenty minutes! The crossing guard and I are now mortal enemies."

While Chris and her mother shared the same brown

hair, Chris had inherited her height from her father. Mrs. Pine compensated for her size by being extra loud.

"It's my fault, Mrs. Pine," Jun offered. "Chris was helping me with something."

Helping him *out* of something was more like it.

Mrs. Pine managed a brief smile. "Hello, Jun." She opened the passenger's side door. "Your hair appointment is at 3:00," she said to Chris. "And Charlene doesn't like to be kept waiting."

"I can't, Mom." Chris said. "Jun and I are . . ."

Mrs. Pine silenced her with a frantic waving of her hands. "Stop, stop, stop! Your aunt's wedding is tomorrow. And there's no way I'm letting my daughter go to church with hair that looks like it was styled with an egg beater."

"But . . ."

"In!" Mrs. Pine demanded.

Chris looked smaller somehow as she ducked into the car under her mother's disapproving glare. Circling back around the front end, Mrs. Pine called to Jun, "You shouldn't encourage her."

"Me? I said she needed a haircut a week ago."

"You've got to be extra loud if she's gonna hear you." Mrs. Pine opened the driver's side door and stuck her head inside the van. "ISN'T THAT RIGHT, DEAR?"

Chris rolled down the window. "This is going to be *fun*," she muttered to Jun.

"I heard that," her mother said, snapping her seatbelt into place.

Chris seized Jun's wrist. "Just promise me one thing."

"What?"

"Don't turn your back on Kimmie. Not even for a second."

Chris's eyes echoed the seriousness in her voice. The car pulled away then, separating their hands. Jun watched the minivan go, feeling somehow smaller without his best friend. Rousing himself, he walked down the sidewalk at half his normal pace. He'd promised Kimmie information. Did he have any worth giving? Sure, he had a list of names. Dion Little, Rachel Cook, and Melanie Stevens. But all of them had alibis. He was no closer to naming the culprit than he was five days ago.

He crossed the teachers' parking lot. The sun hung high in the cloudless sky, while dark shadows pooled beneath the cars. A silver convertible exiting the parking lot screeched to a stop beside him. The driver's side window lowered with an electric hum.

Becky Dent, the part-time librarian and full-time hairstylist, sat behind the steering wheel, smiling at him. The plunging neckline of her form-fitting black T-shirt revealed a wedge of tanned skin that looked out of place in late October. She wore oversized sunglasses with round lenses, giving her face a bug-like appearance. She smelled faintly of hairspray.

"Hey, you," she said sweetly.

"Hello," Jun answered warily, surprised by this unexpected meeting. "What are you doing here?"

"Mrs. Adams is still out. I'm covering for her again."

"She's not still sick, is she?"

"The office doesn't tell me those sorts of things. They just ask if I'm available." Becky Dent pushed her sunglasses down the bridge of her nose and cast furtive glances left and right. "Gotten anywhere with your case?" she asked.

He'd attracted the attention of the real cyberbully, and the whole school hated him. That was progress, right?

"Actually, no," he admitted.

He looked away, embarrassed, and his eyes fell on a book that lay on the passenger's seat of the car. Jun could just barely make out the title: *How to Talk to your Kids*. The book reminded him of his own mother, and that kick-started his forgotten frustration over her unauthorized cyber snooping. Jun considered ordering the same book online and sending it anonymously to his mother. Maybe she'd learn a thing or two about being open and honest with her son.

"I really do hope you find a way to clear your name," Mrs. Dent said.

Jun squinted at her. She was the one who'd given his name to the principal in the first place! "Why are you suddenly so sure that I didn't post the pictures?"

Mrs. Dent removed her sunglasses and looked him up and down. "Honey, you just don't have it in you."

Jun wasn't sure if he should be encouraged by this. If he didn't have the backbone required to commit crimes, maybe he lacked the determination to solve them. But he wasn't given the opportunity to question her further. After a wink, Mrs. Dent drove off, the tires of her sports car screeching, leaving Jun to choke on her exhaust fumes.

* * *

Brookfield's downtown was a blink-and-you'll-miss-it affair: a dozen stores spread over two blocks with a single light to manage the traffic. Large green awnings offered protection from the sun, shading the brick-lined sidewalks. Every thirty feet an ornate black streetlamp rose up and watched over the slow-moving cars with a single whitish-gray eye.

As Jun strode along, his brain attempted to put together enough information to appease Kimmie Cole. The problem was obvious. All his suspects — Leah Armstrong, Dion Little, and Rachel Cook — were in class at the time the pictures were posted. And his most likely suspect, Melanie Stevens, was on the other side of town.

Across the street, a dark shape streaked past the storefronts. The movement caught Jun's eye and he looked up.

Speak of the devil.

Melanie Stevens, cloaked in black from hair to toe, coasted on her bike, weaving slowly around the foot traffic. Melanie parked outside of the post office and chained her bike to a street lamp. She approached a door Jun had never noticed before, sandwiched between the post office and Pablo's Pizza Parlor. Pulling it open, she disappeared inside.

Intrigued, Jun hustled across the street to investigate.

The door had a square glass window. Jun leaned his head against it and cupped his hands over his eyes to reduce the glare. He was just in time to see Melanie step into an elevator. Jun retreated a step and looked up, realizing that there were apartments or offices above the stores. He waited until the elevator doors closed behind Melanie before pushing into the narrow lobby. He watched the numbered bar above the elevator. A bell sounded as it passed each floor. The number three lit up and remained lit.

A steel and glass case mounted on the opposite wall housed the building's directory. All the rooms on the third floor belonged to doctors. Of the three names listed, only one was familiar — Dr. Cody.

Where had he heard that name before? He squeezed his eyes shut as images from the last five days whirled around his head. He had it! Dr. Cody was the man who'd called Mr. Hastings when Jun was in his office yesterday. Jun frowned.

Melanie looked perfectly healthy when he'd spoken to her the day before. What could she have possibly contracted in the last twenty-four hours that would trigger a visit to the doctor's office?

There was no time to ponder the question. Kimmie was waiting. Jun exited the building and turned left at the first intersection, leaving the downtown area behind. Kimmie wanted answers. All Jun could offer was a list of names of people who held a grudge against Kimmie. It was a long list, sure, but would it be enough?

Jun released a shaky sigh. He already knew the answer.

Chapter 18

Jun stood outside Kimmie's front door, unable to make himself ring the bell. He looked to his right at the place where Chris should be standing. Instead, he found only his own stubby shadow. A sense of helplessness gripped him. Doubt crept in behind it. A half hour ago talking to Kimmie had seemed like a sensible move. Now, without the protection Chris offered, it felt more like throwing a T-bone to a hungry lion.

Jun tore open a fresh bag of cheese balls and popped one into his mouth. He held the ball between his tongue and the roof of his mouth, allowing it to dissolve slowly, coating his tongue with cheesy goodness. He repeated the procedure with a second ball, and then a third, but no amount would calm his nerves. A wrong move here could land Jun on Kimmie's list. And the last thing he needed was someone else after him. If Kimmie wanted a piece of him, she'd have to stand in line behind Charlie Bruno, Mr. Hastings, Rachel Cook, and the rest of the Brookfield student body.

A curtain stirred in the bay window to his left. Jun caught a flash of blond hair. Moments later, he heard footsteps, followed by the thunk of the deadbolt. The door opened and there Kimmie stood with one hand on her hip.

"You're late!"

Jun checked his watch. It was 3:37.

"I-I-I'm sorry." Jun said, flustered. "There was another matter I needed to attend to. It's related to your current predicament."

"Huh?"

Chris wasn't there to translate.

"I had to make a stop in town," Jun said. He didn't want to mention his Melanie sighting until he knew why she was at the doctor's office.

"Great, I'm sitting here waiting for the name of the person who destroyed my life and you're out buying cheese balls. Did you get a soda too?"

Jun's jaw worked, but nothing came out. Thirty seconds into their first meeting and already Kimmie had scared him speechless.

"Just get in here." She grabbed his arm and yanked

him inside.

Kimmie was not as tall as he was expecting. Then again, he had expected horns and a forked tail too, but neither was present. Kimmie had extra large brown eyes. On someone else, they'd be striking, maybe even beautiful, but Kimmie's face was narrow, and her cheeks sunken, so those oversized eyes gave her face a cartoonish appearance, like a character from a Japanese Manga novel. A purple sweatshirt, two sizes too big, hung below her waist, giving her a shapeless appearance, and making it impossible to see the reason the pictures were posted.

Jun followed Kimmie into the living room. "Are your parents home?" He did not particularly want to be alone with Kimmie.

"Mom's not home until six," she said. "It's just me and my little sis."

Kimmie stopped beside a large beige couch. She did not invite Jun to sit.

"Okay, so who is it?"

Right to business.

"Um . . . could I have a glass of water?" Jun asked. "I'm a little parched from the walk over."

"Not until you tell me who's behind all this!"

"I'm really pretty thirsty."

Kimmie's nostrils flared. Under normal circumstances, she probably would've told him to tough it out. But these circumstances were far from normal. Jun had information. Information she needed.

With an angry glare, Kimmie stomped off to the kitchen.

Jun explored the living room, hoping that some object — a book, a picture, a framed award — might offer inspiration. He gravitated to the mantle over the fireplace. The fireplace wasn't real. Fake wood crisscrossed the hearth to hide the gas jets built into the brick floor. Above, four family pictures lined the mantle. Jun picked up one that showed a middle-aged woman with shoulder-length blond hair. Kimmie's mom, he guessed. Mrs. Cole and Kimmie posed for the picture cheek to cheek, their grins running together, forming one four-inch smile.

Kimmie had said that her mother would be home at six, but there was no mention of her father. After a quick glance down the mantle, Jun saw that no men were present in the pictures. Mrs. Cole must have taken down the pictures of her husband after the divorce.

Kimmie was suddenly behind him. "Here!"

Jun turned and she thrust the glass in his face. He accepted it with a smile and took a long, slow drink.

"Okay, that's enough," Kimmie said. "You don't want to over-hydrate."

Jun withdrew the glass and wiped his lips with the back of his hand. His attempt to drown the butterflies in his stomach had failed. There were still flapping around in there.

"Who posted those pictures?" Kimmie demanded.

Jun blew out a long breath. He had to go with the truth. It was all he had.

"I don't know."

Lines creased the perfect skin of Kimmie's forehead. "But you said you knew who the cyberbully was!"

"I said I had information," Jun corrected. "That's all."

Kimmie's face turned red. If she were a teakettle, she'd be whistling right now. "I need a name, Jun," she barked. "And you're not leaving until I get one."

Jun scanned the room for possible escape routes.

Kimmie snapped her fingers in front of his face. "Focus!"

"Okay, okay . . . I've been thinking about this on the way over."

Kimmie nodded.

"And I do have an idea. I haven't worked out all the details . . ."

"Just spit it out!"

Dion's whereabouts during block seven had been confirmed by Mr. Wainwright. Rachel Cook's location during that same time had been verified by Chris, who shared the same math class. That left just one person whose alibi hadn't been confirmed.

"Leah Armstrong," Jun said. "She was in science class

when the pictures were posted, but I was thinking . . . what if she got up to use the bathroom? Her class is just down the hall from the library. It would only take a few minutes to sneak over and upload the pictures." The more Jun spoke, the more he warmed to the theory. "According to Mrs. Armstrong, Leah's a computer whiz, so she had the technological know-how to dodge the security protocols and post on the school's website. And," he added, raising one finger in the air, "the 'Feed-Me' picture provided all the motivation she needed."

Jun finished this mini-speech with a brisk nod, impressed by his on-the-spot deduction.

Kimmie slowly shook her head back and forth.

Not the reaction Jun had hoped for.

"You forget," Kimmie said tightly. "I was in school last Friday. And Leah's in my block seven. She was there the whole time!"

Another theory — his best yet — shot to pieces.

"What else you got?" Kimmie demanded.

Jun managed a weak smile, holding out his hands, palms up.

Kimmie looked him up and down. "What a waste of time you are," she said.

Her words stung like a slap across the face. Jun was thinking of ways to excuse himself when a young girl, maybe four or five, appeared in the doorway between the living room and the kitchen. She was Asian. Pigtails bound up with blue rubber bands stuck out from the sides of her head like handlebars. She edged cautiously into the room.

Jun whispered, "Who's that?"

"My little sister," she said like it was the most obvious thing in the world.

"*That's* your sister?"

"Her name's Sun." Kimmie's nose wrinkled. "What're you, a racist?"

Jun was struck dumb. It wasn't often that a guy with a name like Jun Li was accused of being a racist.

"I can't find my crayons," Sun said, pouting.

Kimmie put her hands on her knees. "I'll help you, sweetie." Her voice was suddenly high and feather soft. "Did you look in your room?"

"Uh-huh."

"And under the bed?"

Her pigtails flapped as she nodded.

"Well, they must be here somewhere," Kimmie said. "Come and help me look."

The little girl dropped to the carpet and looked under the coffee table. Kimmie searched between the cushions. Jun checked his surroundings to make sure he was in the same house. The person who'd greeted him at the door was nothing like the girl now lifting up the cushions. The image forced him to reevaluate his opinion of Kimmie. Any kid that was that nice to their little sister couldn't be all bad.

"Jun!" Kimmie called. "Don't just stand there. We're looking for crayons. Make yourself useful."

That was the Kimmie he knew!

Jun checked the bookcase, the console table, and then crossed to a doorway leading off the living room. It was a small office. On the wall, a law degree hung proudly in an oversized, gilded frame.

"Got them!" Kimmie called.

Jun returned in time to see Kimmie pulling a box of crayons from an open drawer in the coffee table. "They're right here, sweetie."

Sun dashed to her sister with an outstretched hand. Kimmie handed off the crayons, then opened a coloring book to a fresh page and placed it on the coffee table. Sun settled herself on the rug, legs folded beneath her. The tip of her tongue protruded as she worked a brown crayon back and forth over a horse chewing hay.

Kimmie smiled at her sister, then led Jun away by the elbow. "Look, I've been cooped up in this house for five days," Kimmie said, her tone softer than before. "There must be something in that head of yours that can help me."

Jun thought about the missing pieces of the puzzle. "Dion Little said he'd never met you. Then I spoke to Mr. Wainwright and he confirmed that you two had several

conversations at the beginning of the year. He even speculated that you might be . . ." Jun couldn't believe he was
about to suggest this to Kimmie Cole ". . . boyfriend and
girlfriend?"

Kimmie's explosive reaction would have made Chris
proud. "Me and Dion?" she half-shouted. "No way!"

"That's what Mr. Wainwright suggested."

Once her outrage faded, Kimmie grew pensive. Soon
she was nodding her head. "I forgot about Dion. It's got to
be him."

"Not possible," Jun said. "He was in English class. Mr.
Wainwright confirmed it."

Kimmie rolled her eyes to the ceiling. "Arrgh!"

"Umm . . ." Jun began cautiously. "Is there something
you're not telling me about Dion?"

"No!"

"Kimmie," Jun said softly, "I can't help you unless you
tell me everything."

Kimmie tucked a lock of hair behind her ear. "We're
on the wrong track," she said. "The person we're looking
for has to be someone who really hates me . . . someone I
know personally. Someone who knows about my . . . uh,
problem."

"The bulimia?"

Kimmie glanced at Sun, then pressed a single finger
against her lips.

"Sorry," Jun said. After a moment of thought, he added, "The person you're describing sounds a lot like Melanie Stevens."

Kimmie snapped her tongue. "Don't you think she's the first one I thought of? But the pictures were posted from a Brookfield computer. And Mel was all the way across town." Kimmie stared at her feet then, not meeting Jun's eyes. "Did you go over there?" she asked, her voice suddenly drained of confidence. "Did you talk to her?"

"Yeah."

"What'd she say about me?" Kimmie asked, peeking up at him.

Jun recapped the information he'd gathered — Melanie's confrontation with Kimmie about her eating disorder, the breach of trust with the guidance counselor, and the retaliation of the text-message attack.

Kimmie held up her hands. "Wait a second! The texting wasn't my idea. It was Leah's. She came up with it."

A piece of the puzzle fell into place with a satisfying thunk. Leah Armstrong played a role in the attack that caused Melanie to leave Brookfield. That explained why she freaked out when Jun plucked the photo from the picture collage. Leah didn't want anyone to know that she was partly responsible for the incident that caused Melanie to transfer.

"It was supposed to be a joke," Kimmie said, her voice

full of regret. "I had no idea every kid and their bratty little sister would text Mel."

Seconds dragged by as Jun formulated his next question. Before he could voice it, Kimmie added, "I wasn't trying to push her over the edge, okay? It just sort of happened."

Jun sensed there was more to this story. He pressed his lips together. Silence was working better than questions.

"Seriously. I had no idea she'd . . ." Kimmie shrugged. "You know."

Jun shook his head.

Kimmie glanced at Sun. The preschooler carefully traced the edges of the horse's hind legs. Turning back, Kimmie held out her hand, palm up. Slowly, she drew one finger over the underside of her wrist.

"Huh?"

Kimmie made the same move, quicker this time.

"I don't get it," Jun said.

A low growl escaped Kimmie's lips. "She tried to . . . you know," her voice dropped to a whisper, "kill herself."

Jun suddenly remembered the black bracelets Melanie wore.

"It wasn't my fault," Kimmie insisted. "Mel was my best friend."

Transferring schools — it made sense. Going Goth — he understood that too. But suicide . . . he couldn't get his head around it. Things for Melanie must have been worse than he imagined.

Thunk! Another piece fell into place. Melanie's attempted suicide in August must have been what forced Principal Edwards into retirement.

Kimmie crossed the room and sat beside her sister on the floor. Sun cozied up to her sister, unaware of the haunted look on her face.

Jun crossed to the couch, intent on saying something comforting. He stopped halfway. He was at a loss for words. He wished Chris were there to help. Then again, Chris probably wouldn't know what to say either, beyond something like, "Walk it off, Cole."

It was during this moment of awkward inaction that the answer came to him. "Wait a second!"

His voice was so out-of-nowhere sudden that Kimmie and Sun both looked up.

"Do you have a smartphone?" he asked.

"Of course." From her back pocket she withdrew the Laser XL2. Apparently Jun was the only kid without one.

She handed it over. The wallpaper picture featured Charlie sporting a goofy grin, with his lacrosse stick resting on his shoulder. Charlie would be pleased to know that he still maintained a prominent place on her phone.

Kimmie caught him staring. "Get on with it!"

Searching for the right words to comfort Kimmie had reminded Jun of his equally awkward conversation with Melanie Stevens. That triggered an image of the uniformed girls from Saint Mary's skipping down the steps at the end of the school day. And when did their day end? At three — a half hour later than Brookfield. That got him thinking — was there anything else about Saint Mary's schedule that was different from Brookfield's?

Jun quickly found his way to the internet browser and looked up Saint Mary's school calendar. "That's it!" he shouted and handed the phone back to Kimmie to show her the proof. "Brookfield School has their staff development days on alternating Wednesdays. Everyone gets out at one o'clock. But Saint Mary's has theirs on Fridays, which means . . ."

"Mel was out of school that afternoon!" Kimmie said. "She had enough time to get to Brookfield and post the pictures."

"I think so."

"Oh my goodness!" she shrieked. "Thank you!"

Kimmie dashed around the coffee table and hugged him, hard.

Jun had never had a hug like this from someone that wasn't a member of his family. Still, he found it impossible to hold onto his hate for Kimmie-the-bully when Kimmie-the-victim was pressed against him. She was not, as Ashley and Koko had suggested, totally evil.

Kimmie released him and took back her phone. "I've got to call my mom," she said, giddy.

The undiluted joy on Kimmie's face was unmistakable. Jun wondered why he didn't feel the same. In just five days, he'd cracked the case. Melanie Stevens now had a large neon sign over her head that blinked: guilty, guilty, guilty. But Jun wasn't so sure. All the evidence fit; it just didn't feel right.

"Kimmie . . ." he began.

She pulled the phone from her ear. "What?"

He couldn't put a finger on exactly what bothered him.

"What?" she asked again, insistent.

Words failed him. He shook his head and shrugged.

Rolling her eyes, Kimmie drifted away as the call connected. "Mom, you'll never guess what just happened . . ."

Feeling suddenly alone, Jun said, "Okay, I guess I should go." When there was no response, he called, "See you later, Kimmie."

She waved at him. If it was a goodbye wave or a don't-bother-me wave, he didn't know.

Jun showed himself out.

Chapter 19

The Gabrielle Street Convenience Store was located just three blocks from Jun's house. Everyone called it the Grab 'n Go because Sandy, the old man who worked the counter, had poor eyesight. High schoolers often walked off with sodas or magazines stuffed down their shirts. Jun, of course, paid for his ice cream cone and sat on the short flight of concrete steps in front of the store.

A few minutes later, Chris plunked down beside him. He'd texted her immediately after leaving Kimmie's house.

"Ice cream in the middle of the day?" she said. "Gonna wash that down with a candy bar?"

"I'm hun . . ." Jun broke off when he noticed Chris's hair. It was several inches shorter and had been styled to hug the curve of her face. She looked . . . pretty. Jun wondered why he'd never noticed before.

"Stop staring," she snapped.

"But it looks real . . ."

"Don't say anything. I hate it."

"Seriously, Chris, it's . . ."

"It's *my* hair. No one else gets to have an opinion."

Jun knew a losing battle when he heard one. He proceeded to fill Chris in on the details of his meeting with Kimmie, including naming Melanie as the culprit.

Chris thumped her thigh with her fist. "I told you it was a girl!"

"You were right," he said, frowning. Now that he'd solved the puzzle, the solution was disappointingly obvious.

"So that's it, right?" Chris asked. "You're off the hook?"

"Case closed," Jun said. "I guess." He stared down at the concrete. It was dotted in places with ancient splotches of blackened gum.

Chris reached over and shook his shoulders. "Come on, relax! You're not getting expelled. We should be celebrating." She popped up. "How 'bout an energy drink? My treat."

Jun barely heard her. "There's just one thing that's bothering me."

Chris plopped back down. "What?" she asked, deflated.

"How could Mel post the pictures from the library

without anyone noticing her? I mean, it's Melanie Stevens we're talking about. She wears more black than Darth Vader."

Chris dismissed the idea with a shake of her head. "Maybe she put on normal-people clothes before coming over. And she probably had a hoodie to cover that jet black hair."

Jun nodded. The rationalizations fit perfectly. And yet Mr. Hastings had been so certain that Melanie had an alibi. Had the principal simply forgotten about Saint Mary's early release schedule?

In the silence that followed, Chris studied the ingredients list on the discarded wrapper. "Do you have any idea what's in this?"

"Too late," Jun said, popping the last of the cone into his mouth. "I'm done."

Shaking her head, Chris balled up the wrapper and shot it at a nearby trashcan. Jun followed the paper ball as it spun through the air and sailed into the can without hitting the rim. When he looked back at Chris, he was struck again by how pretty she looked.

"Your hair really does look nice," he said.

Chris snorted. "Like I care."

Despite her sharp words, Jun spotted a shy smile before she stood and started down the block.

He ran to catch up.

"Have you called Principal Hastings to tell him the news?" Chris asked.

"Not yet. But I will. Soon."

All the information churning in his brain needed time to settle. Once it did, he would reexamine all the evidence one final time before announcing the cyberbully to the principal.

Chapter 20

Saturday

Around 8 a.m., the sun found the right angle and managed to slip around the drawn shade in Jun's bedroom. A brilliant yellow line cut across his face and seeped through his left eyelid, waking him.

Shoving his feet into slippers, he shuffled out of the room, using his fingers to comb his wild hair. One hand on the banister, he thumped unsteadily down the stairs. As he descended, a familiar sound reached his ears: the distinctive double click of a mouse.

Who was the early bird? he wondered.

Jun reached the bottom step and turned into the family room, rubbing his eyes.

What he saw made him freeze. The computer was on. His school email account was open. And his mother was clicking her way through the hundreds of messages in his inbox.

Whatever drowsiness had lingered since getting out of bed instantly evaporated. His heart pounded with an intensity he could hear in his ears.

"H-h-how did you get into my account?" he stuttered.

"I hacked my way in," a voice said from behind.

Jun spun in time to see his father emerge from the kitchen, holding two cups of coffee. Mr. Li walked by his son and handed the second cup to his wife. She accepted it with a whispered thank you.

"Dad," Jun cried, "my account is password protected. That information is private!"

Instead of answering, Mr. Li glanced at his wife. Apparently, she would do the talking. Mrs. Li took a tentative sip from her steaming mug, then stared into it, lost in thought. Years seemed to pass as Jun waited for his mother's first words.

"I trusted you," she said.

The past tense of the verb stung in a very present-tense sort of way.

"B-b-but I didn't do anything."

"I've been asking around about your girlfriend," she said. "The neighbors had a lot to say about Melanie Stevens. She's not the nice girl you made her out to be."

Jun wanted to point out that he'd said nothing about

Melanie's character. It was his parents that made assumptions based on her pictures. Looking again at his mother's rigid posture and pinched lips, he decided it was best to hold his tongue.

"On Monday," she continued, "you told me you didn't know Kimmie Cole. And now I find out that Melanie Stevens is Kimmie Cole's best friend."

"Was," Jun corrected. "They don't hang out anymore."

"It doesn't matter!" she snapped. His mother closed her eyes for several seconds to regain her composure. In a calmer voice she said, "We were worried that you might be mixed up in this situation with Kimmie, and since we couldn't get an honest answer out of you, your father and I decided to look through your email account."

"You can't just snoop around without my permission!" Jun said, raising his voice.

"Look at this inbox and tell me I wasn't justified!" Mrs. Li demanded, pointing at the screen. "Four hundred angry emails!"

Jun winced. The number had nearly doubled overnight.

"All full of hate for my son!"

The sound of her trembling voice pierced Jun's heart. All these problems, they were his, and he would deal with them. But to upset his *mother*, that elicited a new kind of hurt, sharper and deeper than anything he had experienced before.

"Have you read these?" she asked. "According to these letters, you're guilty of spreading rumors, calling girls terrible names, and having posted incriminating pictures of Kimmie Cole." His mother turned in her seat, her dark eyes flashing with anger. "The very same pictures I asked you about on Monday."

"Let's not jump to conclusions," his father said, patting the air to cool tempers. "I'm sure Jun has a perfectly good explanation."

Mr. Li looked to his son, his eyes full of hope.

Jun had a good explanation, he just couldn't share it. To do so would reveal that he was the one accused of exposing Kimmie's secret. Why hadn't he told his parents the whole story on Monday? Sure, his mother would have flipped, but anything was better than this.

Mrs. Li opened another email. "And what's this?" She squinted at the screen. "This one says you're madly in love with Chris Pine!"

"Jun!" his father cried.

Apparently, one girlfriend was good news. Two was unprincipled.

"I-I-I can explain."

But should he? Once he called Mr. Hastings and named Melanie Stevens as the cyberbully, he was off the hook. His mother never had to know what he'd been accused of.

"I'm waiting," she grumbled.

Jun was searching for an explanation (one that wouldn't explain too much) when the phone suddenly rang. Everyone jumped.

"Ignore it," Mrs. Li said.

Mr. Li bent over the caller ID. "It's the school."

Mrs. Li shot Jun a look that said, *What have you done now?*

Jun sputtered, "It-It's probably not important."

Mrs. Li strode past him and snatched the phone from its cradle. She listened to the caller's greeting and then responded, "Hello, Mr. Hastings."

Jun pinched his eyes closed. That name was a punch to the gut.

"Yes," his mother said, nodding, "we were just talking about the pictures. Perhaps you can explain what's been going on this week." She listened some more. "What? Okay, alright . . . if you insist."

Mrs. Li thrust the phone at him. "Mr. Hastings wants to speak with you." An angry glare accompanied her words and drove Jun to stare at his slippers.

Eyes averted, he reached out for the phone, but his shaky hands fumbled it. The phone hit the computer chair and clattered to the floor. Bending, he scooped it up and said quickly, "Hello. Sorry. I'm here."

"Jun, I just got a call from Mrs. Cole. Did you tell

Kimmie that Melanie Stevens posted those pictures?" The principal, as always, was speaking a little too loudly.

Jun held the phone away from his ear. "Yes."

"Didn't I tell you Melanie had an alibi?"

It wasn't a question. And judging from the way he spit out his words, no explanation would be acceptable. Jun tried anyway. "Saint Mary's had an early release last Friday. Melanie had plenty of time to . . ."

"Melanie's whereabouts last Friday have been confirmed and verified. We know exactly where she was."

"Where?"

"You've accused the wrong person," the principal barked. "Put your mother back on!"

Mrs. Li must've heard Mr. Hastings's half-shout. She held out her hand for the phone. Jun reluctantly relinquished the receiver. As he did, he stared at the floor, unable to survive another double-barrel blast of disappointment from his mother. She didn't belong in this world of bulimia and bullies, of accusations and alibis.

"Yes . . . okay . . . I understand." She listened to the principal some more and then shrieked, "What?"

Jun guessed that was the part about him being a suspect in the case.

The conversation lasted another ten minutes with his mother extracting every last detail from Mr. Hastings. She then looked at Jun, her eyes narrowing as if coming to a decision. She sucked in some air through her nose, straightened her back and said into the phone, "Let me make one thing clear, Mr. Hastings. There is no chance my son had anything to do with posting those pictures. And I resent the implication. If anything, you should be thanking him. If what you've told me is true, he's been helping to track down the culprit all week. Contact the superintendent if you must, I'll be on the phone with my lawyer."

The short speech made Jun want to cheer.

Mrs. Li said a hurried goodbye and stabbed the off button. She then turned her fierce eyes, like a blinding spotlight, on Jun.

"Thanks," he said weakly.

His gratitude seemed to make her angrier. "I sided with you because I know that you would never post such pictures. But apparently, you are not above LYING TO YOUR MOTHER!"

Jun fell back a step. He couldn't remember a time that his mother had shouted at him. He looked to his father. Mr. Softy. The peacemaker.

Mr. Li avoided his eyes.

"Why-didn't-you-tell-me-about-any-of-this?" Mrs. Li asked, her words fired off like machine gun bullets.

Jun held up his hands. "I didn't want you to worry."

"Jun . . ." Her tone warned he'd have to do better.

"The principal gave me a week to solve the crime," he

said. "I didn't think you'd have to know."

It was like throwing gasoline on a fire.

"Didn't think *I'd have to know?*"

Jun's chin dropped. The volume of his voice fell too. "I-I-I didn't want you to worry."

His sputtering, conciliatory tone defused some of her anger. In a softer voice she said, "Do you think I'd believe such a thing about my own son? I know you're not capable of something like that. But . . . to lie to me *all week?*" She shook her head. "I thought I could trust you."

"I thought I could trust you, too," he muttered under his breath.

"What was that?"

Jun found the courage to look her in the eyes. "My email is private," he insisted. "You had no right . . ."

"I HAD EVERY RIGHT! And your inbox is proof! You think I'm going to stand by and do nothing while my son is ATTACKED?"

"Jun," his father said, "I think now would be a good time to go to your room."

Jun wanted to argue. He changed his mind when he saw his mother's hands; they were balled into fists and trembling at her sides. Another eruption was imminent. He started up the steps. Halfway up, his mother called his name.

"Did your teachers," she started in a softer voice, "have

any intention of writing those recommendation letters?"

Jun slowly shook his head.

Mrs. Li looked away, eyes pinched. It was the final betrayal.

"I tried to get them to do it," he said, his voice cracking. "They kept putting me off."

Mrs. Li turned her back on him. "I can't talk to you right now."

Wounded, and feeling unsteady on his feet, Jun used the banister to climb the remaining steps.

Chapter 21

Sunday

Jun woke Sunday morning with sore thumbs. His eyeballs were dry too, as if they'd been plucked from their sockets in the middle of the night and replaced with marbles. The aches and pains were a byproduct of Saturday's video-game marathon. Turning on his Xbox was the easiest way to turn off his brain. He didn't want to think about the trouble he'd gotten Melanie Stevens into, or how he was — once again — the only suspect in the case against the cyberbully.

Jun's mother had interrogated him twice the day before. With a seemingly endless barrage of questions, she sucked out every last bit of information from his head with the stubborn persistence of a kid slurping up the remnants of a milkshake. Between these exhausting sessions, Jun scavenged the kitchen for food. He took a leftover burrito from the refrigerator and a mini box of cereal from the cabinets. He also found some cookies in one-hundred calorie packs. He took four of those.

He devoured these snacks in his bedroom. Playing video games in his room was the best way to avoid his parents, who spent the rest of Saturday alternating calls between the school and their lawyer.

Jun rubbed his dry eyes again and tumbled out of bed. He walked unsteadily to his Xbox and switched it on again. It was only when the TV crackled to life and the title screen for *War Hero* appeared that Jun relaxed. As he gripped the controller and started the game, his brain eased into a blissful state of numbness. But it didn't last.

Between levels, his mind flashed back to the field hockey picture of Kimmie, Melanie, and Leah. Their grinning faces were a reminder of happier times. For everyone.

Though he'd been burned by his false accusation, part of him still wanted to solve the mystery. He couldn't, though, not until he unraveled the knot in his brain. It had been lodged there ever since Friday's conversation with Kimmie. He'd missed something. He was sure of it. But until he could figure out what, his brain remained hopelessly tangled. Not that it mattered. His desire to do anything about the mystery slipped away when the next level started, drawing him into the game once more.

At some point, his bedroom door opened. The

rumbling in his stomach told him that it was likely some time after noon. Jun glimpsed his father coming through the door, but did not turn to greet him. Instead, he listened as his father crossed the room, stepping on discarded cookie wrappers along the way. The bedsprings behind Jun squeaked as his father sat down.

"It's taken some time," Mr. Li began, "but your mother and I finally understand the sequence of events from the past week. We wish you had told us in the beginning what was going on, but we see now that Mr. Hastings put you in a terrible position. You were only trying to keep yourself from getting expelled."

Jun paused the game and spun his computer chair around. "I should have told you about the pictures on Monday," he said quickly, wanting peace between them.

"It's alright, Jun. I understand."

Relief washed over him. Leave it to his father to be the reasonable one.

"I wanted to let you know," he continued, "that we'll stand behind you during the entire process. Your mother and I will not see you expelled from school. But I've been talking with our lawyer and he thinks it's best for your case, not to mention your safety, if you stay home until we get all this sorted out."

Jun nodded, thankful that he would not have to return to a school where everyone hated him.

"And I believe," Mr. Li said, turning his gaze to the doorway, "your mother has something she wants to say to you."

And there she was. Arms folded, leaning against the doorframe.

"Mom?" Jun asked, unsure of what would happen next.

With some difficulty, she said, "I owe you an apology."

Jun remained very still.

"It was my idea to go through your email," she said.

He wanted to shout — *I knew it!* He bit his bottom lip instead. He could tell it was incredibly difficult for his mother to make this admission. He didn't want to rub it in her face.

"Your email is private," she conceded. "We should have respected that." Mrs. Li thought for a moment, then added, "I should have respected that." She looked across the wrapper-strewn carpet, searching for the right words to explain. "I know it sounds crazy, but . . . mothers will do anything to protect their kids."

The knot in Jun's brain suddenly unraveled. All the jumbled pieces from the week bounced into the air, intermingled, and then fell perfectly into place. He snatched his phone from the nightstand and examined the field hockey picture. He then looked at his mother, his eyes brimming with excitement.

"What is it, Jun?" his mother asked.

"I know who posted the pictures!"

"Who?" she demanded.

"I can't believe I didn't see it before."

His father stood. "Jun, who is it?"

"I need to call Mr. Hastings. Right away."

Chapter 22

Monday

Chris and Jun strode side by side down the school's main hallway.

"You're really not going to tell me?" Chris said. She'd been pestering Jun all morning for the identity of the cyberbully.

"It's complicated," he said.

"What? You think I can't handle it?"

"It's not that. I'm just a little . . . uh, fuzzy on some of the details."

Chris did a double take. "You had Mr. Hastings get all those people together, and you're . . . *fuzzy?*"

"It'll come to me."

"Your butt's on the line, Jun. You sure you know what you're doing?"

Jun didn't answer. At his request, ten people had been gathered in the library, including the school's resource officer. There was no backing out now. A few times that morning he had thought about making a break for it. He was pleased to find that his desire to name the culprit was stronger than the fear of facing his accusers.

Jun continued down the hall. Ahead, Mr. Hastings stood in front of the library door. Yesterday, Jun had revealed the identity of the cyberbully to him. On the phone, Mr. Hastings had been confident and full of fire. Now, his face was pale, and he kept stealing glances through the library window at the group of people gathered inside.

"Tell me again why I'm letting you do this," Mr. Hastings said.

"Because you're out of time," Jun said. "Mrs. Cole wants the name of the bully, and if she doesn't get it, she's pushing forward with her lawsuit against the school."

"It's risky, Jun. For both of us," he said. "There's not enough evidence. You'll need a confession."

"I know that."

"You think you'll get one?"

"I do."

"How can you be so sure?"

The moment the bully's name occurred to him, all the nagging questions from the past week were instantly answered. More than that — it felt right. The answer was now so painfully obvious, he was amazed he hadn't seen it sooner.

"Because the cyberbully is bursting to tell her side of the story," Jun told the principal.

Mr. Hastings nodded, then looked again through the library window. Jun suspected the principal wanted to pull the plug on the whole operation, but there was no backing out now.

"Alright then," Mr. Hastings said. "Let's get this over with."

"Yes," Chris said, striding forward. "Let's."

"Hold on," Mr. Hastings said, barring the door with his arm. "You're not going anywhere. You're not involved in this case."

"Not involved? I've been watching Jun's back all week. And it's not easy work, keeping him out of trouble. You should be giving me a medal, but I'll settle for a front row seat."

Chris . . . as subtle as ever.

Mr. Hastings appealed to Jun. "I can't let her in."

"But I need her in there," Jun said.

"Why?"

All the responses that presented themselves sounded stupid or corny. He locked eyes with the principal and spoke the only answer that made sense to him. "Because I can't do this without her."

Mr. Hastings threw up his hands in surrender. "Fine. What does it matter? Come on, everybody inside. "

Jun was the first through the door. His arrival was closely watched by the library's occupants. Feeling suddenly shy, he averted his eyes and moved to the right to allow Chris and Mr. Hastings to step inside. When he chanced a look up, he saw many scowling faces. Only Kimmie Cole seemed happy to see him. She stood closest to the door and shot Jun a half smile when he entered. Charlie Bruno, standing beside her, saw this and put a protective arm over her shoulder. Kimmie shrugged him off.

Leah Armstrong was there too. She leaned against the checkout counter, as far as she could get from Kimmie and still be in the same room. Even from a distance, Jun sensed that the basketball player was anxious. When his eyes fell on her, she crossed, uncrossed, and then re-crossed her arms.

In between the girls, Dion Little sat in a rolling computer chair. His frown deepened when Jun stepped into the room. Jun avoided the eighth grader's accusing eyes.

Besides Mr. Hastings, there were six other adults in the room. Mr. Wainwright sat behind a table near the bookshelves. He glanced suspiciously at Jun, then returned to the business of winding his silver wristwatch. Kimmie's mother, Mrs. Cole, sat at the same table. Jun recognized her from the photo on the mantle. She was dressed in a gray suit, her blond hair pulled into a tight bun. In front of her an expensive-looking pen lay on a yellow legal pad opened to a fresh page.

Another adult stood to Jun's right. His silver nametag read "Stackhouse." This was the school's resource officer. Stackhouse was tall, with football-player shoulders and a thick leather belt weighed down with walkie-talkie, hand-cuffs, and gun.

The final three adults sat at a table in the rear — Jun's parents plus their lawyer. Mr. and Mrs. Li had arrived early to consult with Mr. Lynch, who would be needed if Jun could not wring a confession from the cyberbully. In that case, Jun would — once again — be the prime suspect.

Mrs. Cole pointed at Mr. Hastings with her pen. "You said on the phone that you'd learned the identity of the cyberbully."

"That is correct, Mrs. Cole."

"Then what are these two doing here?" she asked, indicating Chris and Jun.

Mr. Hastings introduced them. "Jun is the one who unraveled the mystery," the principal said.

Mrs. Cole studied Jun with small dark eyes, then looked back to Mr. Hastings. "You've got a sixth grader doing your sleuthing?" she asked.

"I'm in seventh grade," Jun corrected. Not that one grade made much difference. Sherlock Holmes, he was not.

"Jun has played an integral role in this investigation," Mr. Hastings said. "With Chris's assistance, he has interviewed every relevant person in this room, except for you, Mrs. Cole. And since he's a student, he was able to obtain information I could not."

"I cancelled a meeting for this, you know," Mrs. Cole said.

"Hear him out," Mr. Hastings said. "I believe you will find his final solution . . . enlightening."

"Fine," Mrs. Cole said, "But I have to be in Boston by nine."

"And my class begins in twenty-two minutes," Mr. Wainwright added.

"We'll have everyone out of here on time," Mr. Hastings promised. He then turned to Jun and patted him on the shoulder as if to say *Good luck . . . you're going to need it.*

All eyes turned to Jun. Overwhelmed by the sudden attention, he stuttered, "I wanted . . . uh . . . I'm here to . . . um . . ." An elbow from Chris jumpstarted his speech. "I know who posted the pictures!"

"Yeah, so do I," Charlie Bruno said. "And I'm looking right at him. He even admitted it online. I've got a printout right here." He held up a crumpled sheet of paper. The same sheet Charlie had launched at Jun's face on Friday.

Kimmie yanked Charlie's arm down. "What did I tell you about that?" she hissed.

Jun exhaled a sharp breath. Convincing the group that he didn't write that letter was the first hurdle. "The print-out that Charlie's holding is a letter where someone posing as me confessed to outing Kimmie Cole."

"If you didn't send that letter," Charlie said, "then who did?"

Jun directed his gaze to the center of the room. "The imposter is Dion Little."

Dion snorted a laugh then started nodding his head. "Yep, that's right. As usual, everything's my fault." He held out his wrists for handcuffs. "Take me away, officer."

"This time it's for real, Dion." Jun turned to Officer Stackhouse and explained, "Dion impersonated me because he knew I'd been meeting with Mr. Wainwright. He was worried I'd uncover the truth."

Mr. Wainwright tapped his fingertips together lightly. "And what exactly is the truth, Mr. Li?"

"That Dion has been selling tests from your class," Jun said.

Dion threw his hands in the air. "Aw . . . come on! What's next? You gonna pin global warming on me, too?"

"Dion updates Mr. Wainwright's website," Jun said, "which means he has access to the school's network. I believe once he had access to the system, Dion found his way into Mr. Wainwright's teaching files."

"Wait a moment," Mrs. Cole interjected, "aren't all

teacher accounts password protected?"

"When a new system is installed," Jun said, "there's a default password assigned to every account. It's usually something simple to remember, like *teacher* or *Brookfield*. If Mr. Wainwright neglected to change the password at the beginning of the year, it wouldn't be hard for someone like Dion to hack his way in."

"Mr. Wainwright," Mr. Hastings asked, "did you change your default password?"

The teacher's face flushed. His red scalp could be seen through his thinning white hair. "Moving all my files onto the computer was your idea!" Mr. Wainwright said. "I cannot be held responsible for the delinquents that weasel their way in."

"All of this is just speculation," Officer Stackhouse said evenly. "Jun, do you have any proof Dion actually stole the tests?"

That was where things got a little fuzzy.

Jun released a shaky breath. "Maybe we can ask someone who bought one of those tests," he said. "Charlie Bruno, was it Dion who sold you Mr. Wainwright's test?"

The eighth grader's mouth dropped wide open. "I don't know what you're talking about. I'm here for Kimmie."

Jun turned back to the English teacher. "Mr. Wainwright, what have Charlie's grades been so far this term?"

Mr. Wainwright scoffed. "I cannot reveal that sort of information."

"Can you at least confirm if Charlie was in danger of failing?"

Mr. Wainwright looked to Mr. Hastings for permission. The principal nodded.

"He was," Mr. Wainwright said cautiously.

"And what grade did he receive on your most recent test?"

Mr. Wainwright chose his words carefully. "Charlie was the only student to receive top marks on that particular test."

Jun turned back to Charlie. "Sounds like you got an A. That's a pretty amazing turnaround, don't you think?"

"It doesn't prove anything," Charlie insisted. "I studied for that test!"

"No, you didn't."

This was Chris. It was clear by the surprised look on her face that she hadn't meant to say anything. The words had unexpectedly kicked their way out of her mouth.

"On Monday morning," she continued, "you told me and Jun that you were on the phone all night with Kimmie."

Jun had forgotten about that. He smiled at Chris as he turned to Kimmie's mother. "Can you confirm that, Mrs. Cole?"

Mrs. Cole's hand froze on the legal pad, mid-word. "Yes, I can," she said. "Kimmie was still talking to Charlie when I went to bed."

"I studied all day *Saturday*," Charlie said. "Did you ever think of that?"

Mr. Wainwright's curiosity had been aroused. "If you studied, then you won't mind taking the test again. Of course, all the questions will be different this time around."

"Yeah, I'll take your test," Charlie said, nodding with a confidence that frightened Jun. "No problem."

Jun had hoped that playing Dion against Charlie would cause one of them to implicate the other. Judging by the victimized looks on their faces, neither kid was ready to crack. Now what?

"Well, Jun?" Officer Stackhouse asked impatiently. "What do you have to say to that?"

Jun's heart knocked against his chest. "I . . . uh, just need a minute."

What he got was five interminable seconds of smothering silence. Sure, he knew who the real cyberbully was, but he didn't have any proof. And why would anyone believe him when Charlie's letter announced to the whole world that Jun was the culprit?

Officer Stackhouse cleared his throat. "Jun, if you can't prove you weren't behind the mass-mailing on Thursday, then I'd have to say that Charlie's letter is pretty convincing evidence."

Jun's mother nudged Mr. Lynch. The lawyer stood. "Mr. Hastings, I'd like to speak to my client for a few moments."

His parents were giving up. Throwing in the towel. His mother was already out of her seat, ready to usher Jun out of the room. Jun appealed to his father with wide eyes. His father looked away and shrugged as if to say, *What can we do?*

Jun refused to be led away by his parents or his lawyer. It would a clear admission to everyone in the room that he was guilty of the crime Mr. Hastings had accused him of one week ago. But he was stuck. He needed some new evidence, but at the moment, all he had was a big pile of nothing.

"Charlie's lying," someone announced suddenly.

Jun's head swiveled in the direction of the voice. Kimmie!

He was completely surprised by this last-second reprieve. But not as surprised as Charlie. The eighth grader's eyes bulged.

"Charlie bought that test last week," Kimmie said. "He told me all about it on Friday night."

"Kimmie!" Charlie cried.

She put one hand on her hip and faced him. "Charlie, just tell the truth. There's no way you'd pass that retake, and you know it. You're caught. Be a man and own up to it."

"I'm not gonna own up to something I didn't do. I'll take that stupid test again tomorrow and prove everyone wrong."

Mr. Wainwright stood. "I can administer the test right now, Mr. Bruno. I hope you won't mind an oral examination."

Charlie's face paled as if the teacher had suggested a body-cavity search.

"Question number one: discuss Atticus Finch's role as a citizen in the town of Maycomb versus his responsibility as lawyer for Tom Robinson."

Charlie blinked three times. "Atticus is the dad, right?"

Mr. Wainwright sighed. "Yes, Mr. Bruno."

For several uncomfortable seconds, Charlie stared at the carpet. Jun could almost see the wheels turning in his head.

"Uhhh . . ." Charlie said, "Can I pass on that one?"

"No Mr. Bruno, you may not *pass*," Mr. Wainwright said with disdain.

"Does this question have anything to do with Boo Radley?"

"No, Arthur Radley does not figure into this answer at all."

That name, however, provided an answer for Jun. It was, in fact, the final piece of the puzzle. The name he'd seen on Dion's screen — Arthur Radley — wasn't a suspect; he was a character in *To Kill a Mockingbird*, Mr. Wainwright's class novel. Jun knew from his internet research that the book was later adapted into a movie.

Charlie's breath quickened and his face reddened. If the eighth grader didn't say something soon, Jun was sure he'd pass out.

"Tell us what really happened, Charlie," Jun said.

"Alright!" he said, throwing up his hands. "Mr. Hastings cornered me two weeks back. He said I'd be kicked off the lacrosse team if my grades didn't pick up. What else could I do?"

"Have you tried studying?" Chris asked.

Charlie's eyes flicked to Dion. "You said nobody'd find out!"

Dion's head tilted back and he squeezed his eyes shut as if he were in exquisite pain. "And no one would have if you'd kept your stupid mouth shut."

"I want my money back!"

"Yeah, good luck with that."

"Enough, boys!" Mr. Hastings shouted. "I'll deal with the two of you later."

Mrs. Cole tapped her pen against the legal pad. "I thought we were here to talk about the crime against my daughter."

An involuntary grin tugged at the corners of Jun's

mouth. He worked hard to suppress it. He was over the first hurdle.

"I was just getting to that, Mrs. Cole," Jun said.

Jun turned to face Leah Armstrong. Following his lead, everyone else in the room did the same.

"I didn't have anything to do with those pictures," she said a little too quickly.

"We'll talk about that in a minute," Jun said. "Let me ask you this first — when did you stop being friends with Kimmie?"

Leah shrugged. "I don't know. Some time in September."

"Isn't that about the same time that Melanie Stevens decided to transfer schools?"

"Sort of. Mel switched schools sometime in August."

"And why did she transfer?"

"I don't know," Leah muttered into her shoulder.

Jun turned to the principal. "How about you, Mr. Hastings? Do you know the reason she transferred?"

"I can't say, Jun. You know that."

Jun turned to his go-to girl. "What about you, Kimmie?"

Mrs. Cole held up her pen to object. "My daughter did not come here to answer questions."

Kimmie stepped forward. "Good grief! Can't anybody tell the truth around here?"

There were so many reasons to dislike Kimmie, and yet at that moment, Jun could not have been more grateful for her.

"Mel tried to . . . kill herself," Kimmie said with some difficulty.

"Don't say another word," Mrs. Cole warned.

Kimmie ignored her. "Mel leaked some information about me, about . . . my eating disorder, so I decided to get back at her by sending a nasty text every ten minutes. But it was Leah's idea to invite the whole school in on it. She texted all our friends, asking them to join in."

"Is that right, Leah?" Jun asked.

The basketball player's bottom lip quivered.

"Leah?" he pressed.

When she lifted her head, her eyes were glassy with tears. "I didn't know that Mel would do that to herself." Leah sounded breathless. "I feel terrible. And I haven't sent a nasty text since. I swear."

"And after that," Jun said, "you and Kimmie had a fight, correct?"

"Yeah," Leah said, wiping her eyes with the back of her hand. "I made a crack about her weight at the mall, and she went ballistic. While I was sleeping, Kimmie wrote 'Feed Me' on my forehead, and then took a picture and posted it up everywhere."

"Around the school," Jun clarified. "Not online, which is something I couldn't understand at first. Rachel Cook's picture was posted online. So why not do the same with your picture?" Jun asked the room. "The answer is simple. Leah was the computer expert. Anyone can post a picture online, but only Leah knew how to make the picture untraceable. So when Kimmie decided to strike back at Leah, she went to the only kid she knew who could help her."

Jun turned again to Dion Little.

Dion didn't lift his head to meet Jun's eyes.

"I didn't help her," he said. "And that's the truth."

"I know, Dion," Jun said. "Kimmie tried a couple of times to get your help during Mr. Wainwright's class, but it's clear that you refused, because Kimmie had to fall back on the old-fashioned way of posting her picture — with paper and tape."

Mrs. Cole threw her pen onto the pad. "So we're back where we started. The only one person left is Melanie Stevens. Why isn't she here, Mr. Hastings?"

The principal huffed. "We've been over this, Mrs. Cole."

"But you still haven't told me where she was that Friday afternoon."

"For legal reasons, I cannot reveal her location. You of all people should understand that."

The moment had finally arrived. It had taken Jun seven full days, but he was finally ready to announce the name of the culprit. He stood straighter, feeling taller, despite the fact that he was the shortest person in the room.

"Um, Mr. Hastings," Jun said, "could the truth of Melanie's whereabouts be known if you had parental permission?"

Mr. Hastings smiled, seeing where Jun was going. "Yes," he said, nodding, "I suppose that'd be alright."

"Then let's ask Mrs. Dent," he said.

"Who's Mrs. Dent?" Mrs. Cole asked, exasperated.

"The school's part-time librarian," Jun explained.

"How would she know anything?"

"Ask her," Jun encouraged.

"But Jun," Chris said, "is she even here?"

"Of course, she is. It's Monday."

Mr. Hastings and Jun exchanged a grin. The principal called, "Mrs. Dent, are you back there?"

The room fell silent as everyone waited. Jun stared hard at the bookcases in the rear where earlier he'd seen a flash of movement between the shelves.

"Mrs. Dent?" the principal called again.

Jun held his breath. If she slipped out the back door, he was sunk.

"Mrs. Dent?" the principal yelled, anger creeping into his voice.

No sound. No sign of movement. Jun pressed both hands against his stomach, which felt like it was infested with crawling insects.

"I'm here," a voice said at last from behind a bookshelf. "Can we talk later? Mr. Henderson's class is coming down block one and I've got to pull a boatload of books on the Civil War."

"That can wait, Mrs. Dent. We need you out here right now."

Mrs. Dent appeared from behind the shelves, carrying books stacked to her chin. She set the books on the counter and turned to the principal, smoothing out imaginary wrinkles in her blouse.

"Mrs. Dent," Jun said, "can you tell us where Melanie Stevens goes every other Friday?"

The part-time librarian's laugh was high and thin. "How would I know?"

"Don't play games," Jun said, his heart pounding with excitement. "I know who you are."

Something changed on her face then. Her eyes narrowed and her painted lips pinched together.

"Tell us," Jun urged. "Where was Melanie?"

Mrs. Dent shook her head, making her blond curls sway.

"If you don't tell, I will," Jun said.

"Fine," she said, nostrils flaring. "On Fridays, Mel sees her therapist, Dr. Cody."

"How could she know that, Jun?" Officer Stackhouse asked.

Mrs. Dent answered instead. "Because I'm Mel's mother!"

There was a collective gasp from the room. Jun wasted no time. He pulled out his phone and showed it to the officer. The field hockey picture appeared on the screen.

"What am I looking at?" Stackhouse asked, taking the phone.

"See the silver convertible car Melanie is leaning against?" Jun said. "It's the same one Mrs. Dent drives. Check the parking lot. You'll see I'm right."

Chris's eyelids snapped wide open. "And her fingernails!" she exclaimed, pointing at Mrs. Dent's hands. "They're just like the ones Melanie had."

"Right," Jun said, "which makes sense since Mrs. Dent owns a salon here in town called *Hair Razors*."

Mr. Hastings added, "I did some checking over the weekend. *Hair Razors* is owned and operated by a Miss Rebecca Stevens. Dent is her maiden name."

Jun also thought of the book on the front seat of her car, *How to Talk to Your Kids*. But he saw no reason to embarrass the hairdresser further.

Mrs. Cole stabbed a finger at the principal. "How could you not know Mel's mother was working in your own school?" she demanded.

Mr. Hastings must have been prepared for that question. He wasted no time with his reply. "I signed off on her application, but I didn't know who she was. It's my first year in the district. I had never met Mrs. Stevens. Her daughter attempted suicide before I took over from Principal Edwards."

Jun began to pace. "So Dion Little was busy stealing tests. Melanie Stevens was with her therapist. And Leah Armstrong gave up cyberbullying after the text-message attack." Jun stopped in front of the part-time librarian. "Which leaves *you*, Mrs. Stevens. You had the opportunity, the motive, and I assume since you worked for the school, you also had access to the network password. You could log onto the school's website and post the pictures without too much trouble."

Mrs. Dent sucked in her lips until they had nearly disappeared from her face. Her whole body trembled with anger.

"And," Jun continued, indignant, "to throw the principal off the track, you blamed me!"

"SOMEONE HAD TO STOP KIMMIE!" she shouted.

Jun fell back a step. The look on Mrs. Dent's face, the naked anger and rage there, silenced even the adults in the room.

"I hear things in this job," she continued, struggling to maintain a civil tone. "And let me tell you, most of it is about Kimmie and all the nasty things she's done."

"My Kimmie gets in trouble now and then," Mrs. Cole replied, "but she's not a bad girl."

"What about the pictures she took of Rachel Cook in the girls' locker room?"

Mrs. Cole looked away. "I don't know anything about that."

"And the text message attack she just admitted to?"

"That was Leah Armstrong's idea."

"Kimmie was responsible and you know it!" Mrs. Dent fell silent for a time. Tears leaked from the corners of her eyes. Her long eyelashes batted them away. "Mel was always such a happy child," she said, her voice quivering now. "But have you seen her lately, Mrs. Cole? She's dyed her hair, and she won't wear anything that isn't black."

Mrs. Cole folded her arms and turned away. "I can't help it if your daughter is overly sensitive."

Outrage robbed Mrs. Dent of her speech. With no other way to show how she felt, she grabbed a book from the top of the stack and flung it at Mrs. Cole.

Her aim was off. The book struck Jun in the forehead, knocking him into a nearby table. Jun's parents leapt from their seats and started over. Chris hauled Jun away as Mrs. Dent flung more books at Mrs. Cole. Officer Stackhouse rushed forward and subdued Mrs. Dent. Black mascara cut crooked lines down her cheeks.

Things happened quickly after that. While Jun nursed

the lump on his forehead, Mr. Wainwright marched Charlie Bruno and Dion Little down to the office. Mr. Hastings instructed Officer Stackhouse to escort Mrs. Dent off the premises. The officer gripped Mrs. Dent's arm above the elbow and led her out of the room. Before she reached the door, Kimmie ran to her.

"Tell Mel I'm s-sorry," she sputtered. "I never meant for any of this to happen."

"It's too late, Kimmie," Mrs. Dent spat. "You've ruined her. Permanently."

Stackhouse guided Mrs. Dent into the hallway then, leaving Kimmie beside the door, head down, lips quivering.

Across the room, Jun's parents gathered around him and Mr. Hastings delivered an enthusiastic pat to Jun's back.

"You did it!" he roared.

"Yes, that was impressive," his father added.

Jun's face was oddly expressionless despite all the commotion.

"Are you alright?" Mrs. Li asked.

"How do you feel, Jun?" Chris added.

Relieved. Elated. Euphoric. And yet there was a lingering sense of remorse for Mrs. Dent and Kimmie. Unable to put these emotions in words, he simply replied, "Hungry."

"Come on down to my office then," Mr. Hastings said,

leading the group out of the library. "I keep some cheese squares in my desk."

"Please, Mr. Hastings," Chris said, following after. "Don't encourage him."

Chapter 23

Tuesday

A light snow fell the next morning. Although the official start of winter was still weeks away, the grass was frosted white and steamy smoke puffed out of Jun's mouth as he approached the school. Chris waited for him beside the double doors.

"A week's worth of detective work and what's your reward?" she called. "You get to come back to this place." She shook her head at the unfairness of it all.

In truth, Jun was happy to be back, especially now that he wasn't a suspect or a sleuth. He was just a regular kid. Mr. Hastings had posted a statement on the school's website explaining that Jun was innocent of all charges. Anyone who harassed Jun, the statement read, would be dealt with severely.

"What've you got there?" Chris asked.

Jun held a large manila envelope. "My private school application."

"I thought the deadline was yesterday."

"Mr. Hastings knows the dean at Wellington. He made a few calls and got me a one-week extension. Mrs. Rabinowitz and Mr. Samuels said they'd have their recommendation letters ready by today."

"That's awesome, right?"

"Right," Jun said without enthusiasm.

Chris studied his face. "Then why do you look like your phone just died?"

Jun didn't have an answer. Ever since he heard about Wellington's state-of-the-art computer facilities, he'd dreamed about enrolling in their one-of-a-kind computer classes. And yet, after his experiences this week, he felt more connected than ever to Brookfield, and especially to Chris. Brookfield might be populated with cyberbullies, but it still felt like home to Jun.

A familiar voice cut through the frigid morning air.

"I need to talk to you."

Kimmie Cole, wrapped in a white winter jacket and red scarf, strode over to Jun. "Wait here," she said to the train of kids following her.

Jun counted at least eight in her entourage. Those incriminating pictures, it seemed, had actually improved

Kimmie's reputation. Now that everyone knew Mrs. Dent was the cyberbully, Kimmie had scored sympathy points. She would still have to account for her actions against Melanie Stevens, but for the moment, Kimmie was not the aggressor. She was the victim. And judging by the number of devotees following her, Kimmie was milking that role for all it was worth.

Kimmie pulled Jun aside. Chris followed.

"Do you think you can get a message to Melanie?" Kimmie asked.

"Uh, I guess," Jun said.

"Just give her this." Kimmie pushed a folded piece of paper into Jun's hands.

"What's it say?" he asked.

"What do you think? I tell her how sorry I am, okay? I never wanted her to transfer schools, I never wanted her to . . ." Kimmie looked away. "You know."

Jun did. And Kimmie would have to live with that shame for the rest of her life.

"Why don't you talk to Mel yourself?" Chris asked.

"Who invited you into this conversation?" Kimmie asked.

"Chris is right," Jun said. "You should talk to her face to face."

"Don't you think I've tried?" Kimmie said. "I've sent texts and emails. I even called her house. She won't talk to me."

"You've got to apologize in person," he said.

"And say what?" Kimmie snapped. "Sorry for being such a crazy bitch?"

Up close, Kimmie looked haggard. Her hair had been combed but only halfheartedly, and her eyes were bloodshot. Mrs. Dent's final words in the library must have robbed Kimmie of a night's worth of sleep.

"It's the only way, Kimmie," Jun said.

"Okay genius, let's say I go over her house. Then what?"

Jun was at a loss. He had solved one mystery, but that didn't mean he was an expert in handing out relationship advice. Dear Abby, he was not.

"Well?" Kimmie demanded.

Jun mulled it over. To his surprise, several answers presented themselves. "Send her an email. Tell her you're coming over. Give an exact time and date. Don't ask if you can. She'll say no. Just arrive on time and knock on her door until she lets you in."

"But what do I say?"

"You're still in counseling, right?"

Kimmie stared down at her fur-lined boots. "Yeah, so?"

"Melanie is too. That means you've got something in common. Start there. If you talk long enough, she'll lower her defenses, then just keep apologizing until she forgives you."

Jun was impressed by his own spontaneous advice. So was Chris. She stared at him as if he had just materialized out of thin air.

Kimmie's expression was even more interesting, though. The creases on her forehead and around her eyes thinned, then disappeared. "Okay," she said, nodding, "I'll try that."

A week ago, Jun was convinced that the best way to survive middle school was to keep his head down. No unnecessary contact with teachers or eighth graders. And yet, here he was giving advice — good advice — to the school's most infamous cyberbully. What a difference a week makes! Jun handed back the note and Kimmie accepted it. She had taken only two steps away before she looked back and smiled. "See you around, Jun."

The train of kids following Kimmie also spoke to Jun as they passed. Some said, "Take it easy, Jun," others "Later Jun," and a couple just gave him a nod, an acknowledgement that for the first time Jun was a blip on their radar screens. He registered. He mattered.

Chris held out her hands, palms up. "What am I, invisible?"

Jun rolled back his shoulders. "Looks like things are about to change for me around here. I'm finally going to get some respect."

One girl detached herself from the end of the line. Jun immediately recognized the orange hair. Olivia! The very same girl who'd predicted a week ago that Kimmie would squash him.

Without a word, Olivia grabbed Jun's arm and dragged him to a corner beside the dumpster. A pungent odor wafted down, forcing Jun to breathe through his mouth.

So much for getting respect, he thought.

"Everybody's been telling me what you did for Kimmie," Olivia said. "They say you're the only person who can help me."

A new case was the last thing he needed.

"Sorry, I'm not interested," Jun said.

"You *have* to help me," Olivia said. "I lost my necklace."

"What's the big deal?" Chris said, appearing by Jun's side. "Buy a new one."

"It wasn't actually *my* necklace. It was my mother's. And it wasn't just any necklace. It's a family heirloom. It's not supposed to leave my mom's bedroom, but it matched my outfit so well that I, you know, borrowed it."

"You mean you stole it," Chris said.

"I was planning on bringing it back, okay? Anyway, I opened my locker yesterday between classes and it was gone. My mom's gonna flip. You have to help me."

Jun was still frazzled from his week-long ordeal. But there was something tantalizing about a new case. It called to him the same way his video games did on a rainy afternoon.

Jun looked to Chris, silently asking for her advice. She smiled and shrugged her shoulders, as if to say *it's up to you.*

"Will you help me?" Olivia begged. She looked from Jun to Chris and back again. "Your girlfriend can help if she wants to."

Jun winced. That single word was sure to light Chris's short fuse. Much to his surprise, Chris said nothing. That was a sort of progress, wasn't it?

"Well," Olivia pressed. "What do you say?"

Jun rubbed the lump on the front of his head. It had started to throb, perhaps warning him not to get involved. He weighed his options, and then nodded once, coming to a decision. Jun pulled out a bag of cheese balls, tore it open, then popped one ball in his mouth and chewed thoughtfully.

"Tell me more about this necklace," he said.